VAN HELSING R.I.P.

VAN HELSING R.I.P.

THE DAYWALKER CHRONICLES™ BOOK 2

THEOPHILUS MONROE

MICHAEL ANDERLE

DON'T MISS OUR NEW RELEASES

Join the LMBPN email list to be notified of new releases and special promotions (which happen often) by following this link:

http://lmbpn.com/email/

LMBPN Publishing
PMB 196, 2540 South Maryland Pkwy
Las Vegas, NV 89109

Version 1.00, April 2023
ebook ISBN: 979-8-88541-796-9
Print ISBN: 979-8-88878-349-8

THE VAN HELSING R.I.P. TEAM

Thanks to our JIT Readers

Christopher Gilliard
Wendy L Bonell
Diane L. Smith
Dorothy Lloyd
Jeff Goode
Billie Leigh Kellar
Jan Hunnicutt
Angel LaVey

Editor
The SkyFyre Editing Team

I followed Dracula through the broken doors of the abandoned building that had once housed the Hospital for the Insane of Louisiana in Rapides Parish. Many of the buildings on the grounds were still in operation, but this one hadn't been touched in decades.

Dylan and two other unshifted wolves from his pack followed us inside.

"All right, Venkman, where are the ghosts?"

Dracula turned back to me with narrowed eyes. That old fart of a vampire really did the death-stare well. "This isn't a joke. When the ghost of Abraham Van Helsing comes back, you'll thank me for this."

I raised an eyebrow. "How is hunting a few ghosts in an abandoned asylum going to help us stop someone like Van Helsing?"

"Do you really think we stand a better chance against him with no experience dealing with ghosts?"

I snorted. "I wouldn't say I have *no* experience. I've met a few."

Dracula shook his head. "Those weren't troubled or vengeful spirits. This place is full of them."

"How do you even know that?"

"I searched the interwebs! This place is definitely haunted."

Dylan chuckled. "The interwebs, huh?"

I cleared my throat. "You realize, paranormal groups come into places like this all the time. They rarely find much."

"I know a few tricks. I'll coax the spirits out."

"You'll *coax* them out?"

"Spirits require energy to manifest. Watch your phones. They'll try to drain your batteries. Pay attention to cold spots. Heat is another form of energy they'll use."

I rolled my eyes. "The whole place is drafty. I'm not putting a lot of stock in cold spots. And my phone is old. Battery-drain is par for the course."

"All I need is a sign that a ghost is attempting to manifest. Then, I'll give it a little extra juice."

"You're talking about magic?"

"Straight from the Scholomance. I've got it in spades. So does Abraham Van Helsing. If he comes after us, he'll have all the energy he needs to do whatever he wants."

The building was dusty. No one had cleared the place of cobwebs in years, and the chandelier over the foyer was covered.

As we walked through the property, the floors creaked with every step. I wasn't sure the place was entirely safe, but unless we fell through the floor and happened to impale ourselves through the heart on a broken floorboard on the way down, we weren't in any real danger.

I coughed in my hand. The dust in the air was almost as thick as the layer that covered everything in the place.

Dracula pulled a small device from his pocket and turned it on. He moved it through the air in front of him.

Dylan leaned in to peer at it. "What is that?"

"I think it's an EMF detector. Dracula's probably seen too many episodes of *Ghost Hunters*."

We followed Dracula through the rooms, most of which were

old patient rooms with numbers over the doors and small metal bed frames.

I traced my hand over a dust-covered wall behind one of the bed frames. The initials B.W. were carved into the plaster.

Dracula's EMF detector beeped and flashed a red light. "Something's here."

In a snap, the temperature of the air dropped at least ten degrees.

I stepped back toward the door. When I did, the bed frame slid across the floor and crashed into the opposite wall.

Dracula extended his hand and released a white light, energy from the Scholomance, into the room.

The bed flew at me and I raised my hands to force it back to the floor. Without my vampiric strength, it would have knocked me over.

A dark human-shaped figure appeared in the room. It turned toward me and ran straight through me, knocking the wind out of my lungs.

Dracula stepped aside and laughed.

"What the hell, dude?"

Dylan and the others took off down the hall like scared puppies, and I stepped out into the hall. The energy Dracula released had fueled more than the bed-throwing body-chilling spirit that had struck me. Dozens of specters jetted down the hall. Their ear-piercing shrieks sounded from every direction.

I did my best to dodge the ghosts as they flew at me. I didn't want another one to move through me. That chill was like someone had staked me with an icicle. It didn't do any harm, but it was uncomfortable as hell. Sort of like getting patted down by TSA agents at an airport, and almost as creepy.

Dracula reached into his cloak and grabbed a short rod. Usually, if a guy opens a cloak and pulls out a rod, I'm covering my eyes and running away. As Dracula swung the rod in his hand

—okay, get that visual out of your head—the spirits dissipated on contact.

He was moving down the hall casually, like a stroll through the cereal aisle at the grocery store. He wasn't the least bit terrified. If anything, he was curious about the variety of spirits presenting themselves as we moved through the building.

Dracula reached into his cloak again and handed me a small cylindrical canister of salt. "Pour a line down the middle of the hall."

"Why? What is this going to do?"

He looked at me with a straight face. "We're a-salting some ghosts!"

I groaned. "This really works?"

"Salt is to ghosts as citronella is to mosquitoes. They hate the stuff. Won't cross the barrier. The salt neutralizes the energy they need to manifest. Iron does the same thing. The ghosts I dispatched already will rematerialize somewhere further down the hall, and the salt will contain them in the back of the house."

I poured a narrow line of salt across the hall. A few spirits behind the line were still swirling around, but they weren't charging at us anymore. I pulled out my phone to take a picture. No one would believe it, and they'd think I faked it. Still, if you see a ghost, if you can't capture it with one of those ghostbuster traps, the next best thing is with a photo.

My phone was dead. "Damn it. Think the ghosts drained it?"

Dracula's eyes darted back and forth. "We came prepared. A salt *and* battery!"

I stared hard at Dracula for a few seconds. "Your joke doesn't work. Ghosts *like* batteries. They don't like salt."

"Mice like cheese, but they don't like traps. The same principle applies. We lure them out with energy they can use, then we trap them with salt while we figure out what we're dealing with."

"They're ghosts, Drac. Not much to figure out."

Dracula shook his head. "This is why we're doing this. These are ghosts who don't have a grudge against us at all. They're a bit wily. I suppose it makes sense. These spirits reside in an old asylum. They aren't necessarily out for blood."

"Speaking of going out for blood. I could use a pint of B-positive right now."

Dracula nodded. "Getting struck by a spirit can take a lot out of you. It makes sense you'd be hungry. We have plenty of blood back at headquarters."

The chandelier over my head in the entryway shook. Dracula shouted, "Get out of the way!" as the plaster in the ceiling cracked.

I jumped away just before the chandelier crashed to the floor. "I thought you said these ghosts were harmless. They didn't have a vendetta against us!"

Dracula nodded. "Lesson learned. If these spirits are dangerous, imagine encountering one with all of Abraham Van Helsing's skill and magic who *wants* you dead?"

I shook my head. "We don't know that he'll come after us. Yeah, I beheaded one of his sons. But come on. The guy had it coming. He'd already lived well beyond his years. Plus, we found his youngest son and brought him back to him so he could be saved. Abraham should be grateful."

"I wouldn't count on it. Abraham Van Helsing's ghost tolerated us at the Scholomance because he had no choice. We were pursuing the path of light. That man wanted nothing more in life than to eliminate me."

"You weren't the one who killed his son. You took Samuel back to him at the Scholomance. I spent some time talking to him while you were pursuing the path of light. He wasn't a bad guy. A bit lonely, but now he has Samuel."

The door to the building blew open and created a vacuum that blew my salt line away. "Well, ain't that the balls."

Dracula tilted his head. "The what? Nevermind. We should get out of here. These ghosts might not have a *personal* vendetta against us—if they're ghosts at all—but I'm beginning to suspect we aren't exactly welcome."

"We're investigating ghosts at an abandoned insane asylum, and you expected they'd welcome us with a calm and rational response?"

Dracula grinned. "At least you know a little more about what we might be facing. And we have a great place to train."

CHAPTER TWO

The worst thing about using an old school building for a base was that it had classrooms. That, and rodents. One giant black rat in particular was especially creepy. He poked his head out from time to time, but he was clever. He always found a way back into the walls before we could catch him.

The building was a den for werewolves before Dracula and I showed up. Dylan's pack was small. Between our fight with the Weird Sisters and the Van Helsings, not to mention the other rogue hunters who'd swarmed New Orleans in recent weeks, Dylan's pack was down to three, including himself. All males. This den was a sausage fest, each man's ego more fragile than the last.

Dracula paced across the front of the room, and I tapped my fingernails on my fangs as I listened to him drone on about what he was still convinced would be our next supernatural threat: the vengeful spirit of Abraham Van Helsing.

It had been nearly three months since I'd killed one of his sons, James. He'd been alive a lot longer than any human should due to the immortality elixir the Van Helsing brothers had developed. I spared Abraham's youngest son, Samuel, who'd been posing as a candidate for office. He deserved to die more than any of them, but when I took an ethereal vacation through hell and to the Scholomance where I met the ghost of Abraham Van Helsing, I promised him I'd bring his son back to him so he might be "redeemed" from the path of darkness.

Samuel Van Helsing—later known as "The Carver" (his serial killer name) and later still as the politician, Dean Carver—was abducted by vampires as a child. They turned him and raised him as one of their own, and Abraham Van Helsing had lived the rest of his life believing Samuel was dead.

In the void where Abraham Van Helsing's ghost resided, a version of the Scholomance mystically connected to the actual Scholomance in Romania, time passed differently. Here, it had been a few months, but Van Helsing might have had years to stew over all he'd learned once we sent Samuel back to him. Would he be grateful we gave him a chance to know his youngest, or would he be pissed I'd killed another of his boys? The fact that I was a vampire, not to mention teamed up with Abraham's lifelong nemesis, probably didn't help.

Dracula pointed with a stylus to four different "kinds" of haunts, ways that ghosts might manifest, on his chalkboard: residual, intelligent, poltergeist, and inhuman. "Who can tell me which of these three best explains our experiences last night."

I snorted. "Do I seriously need to raise my hand?"

"You're already speaking."

"Right. Well, I think that's too simplistic. Of those four, only one of them is actually a ghost. Residual haunts look like spirits, but it's more like a psychic energy and intense memory recorded in the ether that plays itself over and over again. A woman walking up and down the stairs. A person reliving their death over and over."

"How do we know they aren't spirits trapped doing those things over and over again?"

"We don't know anything for sure. I've had my encounters

with human spirits. They might be attached, connected, to something, but I don't know that I've ever met one who is really trapped like that."

"What about poltergeists?" Dylan asked. "There were quite a few bangs and odd noises, things moving about."

I shook my head. "Again, not spirits. Not exactly. Poltergeists are created by *living* spirits. A manifestation of some kind of troubled psychological energy."

Dracula nodded. "It's true. They are not former human spirits, but the offspring of living men and women. That doesn't mean they're not intelligent or dangerous."

I sighed. "If we were dealing with poltergeists, they'd been there a while. We were in an old asylum. Troubled psychological energy goes with the territory. But a lot of people also died in the asylum."

Dracula nodded. "It is quite possible that we were dealing with both. A troubled mind, meeting an untimely death, might produce a poltergeist as he dies. The poltergeist can terrorize the human spirit indefinitely should the ghost refuse to go with the reapers."

I shrugged. "Does it matter? Intelligent spirits and poltergeists respond to the same weapons. Iron and salt."

Dracula cleared his throat. "Correction. Their energies can be temporarily disoriented by salt and iron. To properly place a human spirit at rest, whatever ties them to this world must be destroyed. When it is, their names will appear again to the reapers, and they'll arrive to harvest the soul."

"How do you kill a poltergeist?" Dylan asked.

Dracula grimaced. "That's more complicated. The first step is usually to identify the human responsible for the poltergeist's existence. It's not strictly necessary, but it's difficult to discern the second step otherwise. The second step requires pacifying the particular angst that fueled it when it was born. A task much simpler if the poltergeist's maker still lives."

I raised my hand. "So if the person who made the poltergeist created it out of rage, you have to calm them down?"

"Not exactly. If someone births a poltergeist out of rage, they must make peace with the source of their anger. If they do, the poltergeist's energy will fade and die. If birthed out of fear, they must overcome their fear."

"And if the person who made the poltergeist is already dead?"

"If the spirit remains on the earthly plane, the same principle applies. If one can contact the spirit, it's possible to help the spirit overcome their angst."

"And if that spirit has already moved on?"

"Then there is no way to pacify the spirit's angst. Even if the spirit is at peace in the beyond, the poltergeist will continue to act out the spirit's original angst unless the spirit is brought back to the earthly plane."

"That's possible. Zoey and I did that with Roy when we brought him out of Hades and put his spirit into the body of a golem. Now he's the boatman of the River Styx. They say destiny is a cruel mistress. I say she has a sense of humor."

The vampire moved on. "The other method to eliminate a poltergeist is to create one yourself. A poltergeist can kill another poltergeist."

"That can't be easy. Aren't poltergeists usually created by accident?"

Dracula beamed, and I felt like a star pupil. "There's a spell. One I learned in the Scholomance. It's painful. One needn't be a master of the Scholomance to do it. One only need have a soul. Then these words must be spoken."

He wrote words in Greek letters on the chalkboard, and an English transliteration beneath it: *egeire, pneuma anchous.*

"Do not say it aloud. It means 'arise, spirit of angst.' If your angst is focused on the poltergeist, it will destroy the poltergeist you seek to kill. Once it is done, provided your angst was channeled *solely* against the poltergeist, the entity you birth will die with the poltergeist it kills."

I was impressed. "Did you learn all this shit about ghosts and haunts in the Scholomance?"

He shrugged. "And from experience. When a vampire kills and drains a victim, many of those spirits die with angst. Sometimes, poltergeists emerge. If the spirit does not go with the reapers, vengeful ghosts remain. I've handled my share of both sorts over the years."

"What about inhuman haunts?" Dylan pressed.

"I don't think that's what we were facing at the asylum," Dracula said.

"Probably not," I agreed. "But in the spirit of learning, what can you tell us about those?"

Dracula sighed. "They're the most dangerous sort. They are beings who are native to the astral realm but also can interact with the earthly plane. Demons are one sort. The most dangerous. There are also sprites, faeries, and even disembodied gods. There are methods to deal with such things. Exorcisms and the like. Such methods are not always reliable."

"There's also Zoey," I reminded him. "She can reap creatures like that."

"Yes, of course. Let us hope if we ever encounter something like that, she'll be nearby and willing to help."

"Well, thankfully, if your fear is correct. If Abraham Van Helsing comes back as a vengeful spirit, he's very much human."

"And also a master of the Scholomance. There's no telling what sort of creatures he might summon as instruments of his rage," Dracula pointed out.

"Can a ghost create a poltergeist?" I asked.

"It's possible," he allowed.

"But Van Helsing is a master of the path of light. Surely he wouldn't call forth demons or anything nasty like that."

Dracula shook his head. "The path of light isn't so different than the path of darkness. It's but a mirror image. The difference between paths is not so stark as the divide between good and evil. One can work through either path to do great good or great evil. Even then, it's not always clear what's right or wrong. Justice is often exacted alongside vengeance. When kings and governments kill, we call it justice. When individuals do so, we call it murder. But what if the king's or judge's motives are less pure than the individual who takes a life of his own accord? Tyrants throughout history have committed many atrocities and genocides. Who would fault an individual who took it upon himself to execute such a tyrant?"

"Heroes and villains only exist in the comics," I pointed out.

Dracula pointed at himself and grinned. "You're looking at history's perennial villain. We make villains of those we fear, and heroes of those whose valor supports our interests."

I nodded. "Even vampires can be heroes."

Dracula bowed his head. "And virtuous men, heroes of old like Van Helsing, can easily be villains. It's choice, not nature, that makes us one or the other."

CHAPTER THREE

I'd hoped that the trip to the asylum was a one-off. A chance to familiarize ourselves with what ghosts could do and how we might stop them *in case* we ended up facing off with Abraham Van Helsing.

I still wasn't convinced he'd attack. Yeah, we'd killed James Van Helsing—the Van Helsing brother most responsible for his siblings' experience wielding magic of various sorts. In truth, Father Abraham's many sons had become more like the monsters he used to hunt than human. People assume that it's the desire to drink blood that makes vampires monsters. For some of us, that's true. For many vampires, it's *immortality* that makes them something *other* than human. After centuries of death, losing everyone that tied them to their earthly lives, and seeing all the evil committed at the hands of humans, immortality drives a wedge between oneself and one's humanity.

Dean Carver, a.k.a. Samuel Van Helsing, told us as much. They'd aligned with the Weird Sisters to overthrow the world's governments not because the Van Helsings were suddenly cozy with vampires, but because they shared a perspective on the world that saw more injustice and more bloodshed committed by humans and their governments than all the so-called monsters combined.

Alexander and Reginald Van Helsing were still out there. We hadn't encountered them in months. Still, given that they were a flesh-and-blood threat with more than enough reason to hold a grudge against us, Dracula's disproportionate preoccupation with *dead* Van Helsings was bothersome.

Technically, Samuel wasn't dead. We delivered him to the Scholomance in the void to his dead father while he was still breathing. I was more worried that he might come back and, as a vampire, use the sire bond that he'd used to turn the president of the United States to re-launch his original plan.

We had taken Samuel to Abraham in the Scholomance precisely because Abraham believed he could help his son and lead him down a nobler path. That Dracula had turned from his villainous ways meant that it was possible that Samuel could be reformed. Was it likely? Who was I to say?

Dracula's history with Abraham Van Helsing explained much of his fear. Dracula was concerned that rather than Abraham turning Samuel to the "light," Samuel might tempt Abraham "dark." Presumably by revealing that I'd beheaded James. Now that some months had passed, I was beginning to think that we should have been up front with Abraham about what had happened. We could have explained the situation. Anything Abraham might have learned about the incident since then would have come from Samuel.

Given Dracula's experience dealing with Van Helsings, I couldn't dismiss his concerns out of hand. He'd evaded Abraham's attempts to kill him for years—largely on account of his clever booby traps. Alexander and Reginald couldn't show up at the schoolhouse without us knowing it. Their immortality elixir ensured that none of the traps would kill them on the spot, but the darts activated by pressure plates under the floor, trip wires that triggered blowtorches, and intense electrical current running through the windowsills would at least slow them down and give us a chance to apprehend if not kill them before they got inside. How do you kill an immortal Van Helsing? Beheading alone wasn't enough unless we separated the head from the body. To make it permanent, we could smash their heads.

None of those traps would prevent a ghost from infiltrating the property. To do that, Dracula had us mix salt with paint and spread it on the exterior walls. The problem was that ghosts could pass through matter. They weren't bound by the laws of physics. A clever spirit—like Abraham Van Helsing—could still float in from the ceiling or through the floors by passing through the ground below. All he'd need was a single crack, and his entire ghastly form could rematerialize inside the building.

It was a lot like trying to mouse-proof a house. No matter how many gaps you think you close, they always find a way in. At least with salt covering the walls and as much of the ceilings and floors as we could manage, the ghosts would have limited options for entry or exit.

While Dylan, along with his fellow werewolves Logan and Ian, were painting the place, Dracula had me working the computer. My task was to identify any patients who'd died at the old mental hospital. Dracula wanted to go back. He wanted a plan to put those spirits to rest. Considering that we could have been dealing with both intelligent ghosts *and* poltergeists, it was a tall order.

To complicate things, we were also a night away from a full moon, which meant Dylan and the wolves would have to leave for a couple of nights. They were tame wolves, relatively speaking, and they wouldn't kill anyone. Contrary to popular belief, most werewolves weren't homicidal. Leave them in the presence of humans, though, and it was like leaving a child in a room with a candy bowl and telling him not to eat any. Werewolf bites were also problematic for vampires. Since Dracula had mastered the Scholomance, he could protect himself from the effects, but I didn't have that luxury. One bite would leave me in a state of paralysis for a century. If I was lucky, it would also leave me unconscious, but that wasn't always the case. Dracula knew of vampires in the past who had been fully awake for a century but couldn't move after an encounter with a werewolf.

For that reason, vampires and werewolves didn't often team up. Then again, we weren't your run-of-the-mill vampires.

I wasn't worried about what Dylan and the wolves might do while out for the night. They usually retreated to one of the nearby bayous and hunted small game, maybe the occasional alligator. What had me anxious was that two of the Van Helsing brothers were out there. We didn't know for sure that the Van Helsings were responsible, but two full moons back, hunters had gone after them. Dylan, Logan, and Ian escaped.

The next month, Dracula went out with the wolves and they went to a different swamp to the northwest of New Orleans. Now that Dracula had left the dark path for light, he used his power of the Scholomance to take the form of a white songbird. It wasn't as ominous as the bat-form he used to take but, in some ways, it was better. No one would give a second thought to a songbird perched in a nearby tree or flying overhead. Bats, on the other hand, draw a lot of attention.

My research on the asylum didn't turn up much information. I was able to find a few old newspaper articles about the property, and a few of the doctors who worked there around the turn of the century were mentioned. It was something to go on. If we learned a little about the doctors who practiced there, we might be able to uncover the kinds of treatment that the patients in the asylum endured.

Nothing about those doctors or their methods was detailed in what I found. I didn't find patient names, which, despite being pre-HIPAA, wasn't surprising.

We each claimed one of the classrooms as a bedroom. It was a big school with room to spare. I found Dracula in his room, cross-legged and meditating on the floor. He'd tried to teach me to do the same. It was helpful for managing one's natural vampiric urges. I gave it a shot, but I couldn't clear my mind. It's crazy how difficult it is to sit and do or think *nothing*.

I heard a squeak and turned just in time to see that damned black rat disappear into a crack in the walls.

Dracula heard me come in. He probably heard the rat, too, but he didn't flinch a muscle. I stood there for about thirty seconds before I loudly cleared my throat. He ignored me.

I sighed. "Do you want to hear about my research or not?"

Dracula opened his eyes. "Sit with me a moment."

I had several sheets of paper I'd printed off from the internet. Copies of old articles, mostly. I set the papers in front of Dracula and sat on the yoga mat he used for meditation.

"When your mind is clear, when you're in a proper meditative state, you can sense the presence of nearby spirits."

I tilted my head. Back in Kansas City, Zoey and I had worked with a medium named Delphine who'd quickly become part of our team. She had ways of contacting the dead. She was the only *genuine* medium I'd ever met. She not only spoke to the dead, but to other spirits, oracles sent by the gods as mediums between the deities they served and the mortal world. She'd never once suggested meditation as a worthwhile technique to speak to ghosts.

I wasn't sure how effective Dracula's technique would be, but I'd learned before that questioning Drac's expertise was ill-advised. For an ancient vampire, his ego was as fragile as a porcelain doll. It was easier to entertain his ideas and see how things played out. Over the years, Dracula had accumulated a lot of experience *and* superstition. Sorting out which was which was almost impossible.

I kicked off my flip-flops and crossed my legs. "You know I suck at this, right?"

"You do suck."

"Excuse me?"

"We both do. We're vampires."

I chuckled. "You've got jokes today."

"I've always got jokes," he assured me. "I've been thinking about becoming a sit-down comic."

"I think they're called stand-up comics."

"I'm sitting now. Why should standing up be a funnier posture than sitting?"

"Was *that* a joke?"

"Funny, right?"

"Hilarious. I'd say don't quit your day job, but you know, I don't think you've ever had one."

"My day job has generally been sitting on my ass inside. You do have a point. Now that you've made me a daywalker like you, perhaps I could pick up a few odd jobs during the day."

"Why? You're loaded. No need to get a job."

Dracula shrugged. "Because I can. There's a whole world open to me now that I've never considered. If not a job, maybe a hobby."

"A hobby would be good," I admitted.

"Close your eyes. Breathe in and out. Focus on your breaths. Think of nothing else."

I followed Dracula's directions. I inhaled slowly. I held my breath for a second before I released it. My stomach growled.

"I'm hungry."

"Ignore that for now. There's bottled blood in the cafeteria."

I drew in another deep breath and exhaled. "Are you going to look at my research?"

Dracula cleared his throat. "I looked up ADHD on WebMD. They illustrated the concept with a photograph of you."

"Funny. Told you. I suck at this."

"You're not even trying. Stop talking and give it an honest try."

"Sorry."

I resumed my deep breathing. I made it about a minute when my phone dinged in my pocket. I tried to ignore it, but it didn't work. I had to check it.

"What is it?" Dracula asked.

I shrugged. "It was an alert from my news apps. I'm following any stories dealing with the Dean Carver missing-person case."

Dracula raised an eyebrow. "No new developments, I presume."

"Not really. When a man elected to public office disappears the day after he won an election, it isn't surprising that it would be a major news story. Politicians are arguing about whether a new emergency election should be held or if the governor should appoint a replacement to Lieutenant Governor."

"The governor is from the opposing party. It's not a surprise there'd be a fight."

"Want to try this again?" I asked.

Dracula grinned. "Another time. You're clearly not focused."

"I want to show you my research."

Dracula picked up the papers I'd printed and examined the articles. "This is good work."

I shrugged. "Not sure how helpful it is."

"It's a start. Even if you could hack into medical records, these spirits go back too far. They aren't going to digitize patient files from a century ago. I'll have to go there tonight and dig into the records myself."

"You're going to break into the hospital?"

Dracula shrugged. "I can teleport over short distances."

"Are you sure you have to do this tonight? It's a full moon."

Dracula nodded. "Go with the wolves yourself. Use your brooch and follow in the astral plane. You'll be safe from the wolves and if any hunters show up in the swamp you'll be able to deal with them more efficiently than I could."

"This asylum isn't a priority. Right now, the wolves are."

"Anything that allows us to get more experience dealing with spirits *is* a priority, Sienna."

"Hunters are a real threat. They've come for the wolves before. They'll certainly be out tonight knowing it's a full moon."

"Are you suggesting that the spirit of Van Helsing isn't a threat?"

"That's exactly what I'm saying. We have no reason to believe he's coming after us any time soon."

"I know Abraham. He will make a move. It's not a question of if, but when."

I shook my head. "Whatever. Do what you need to do. I'll go let Dylan know I'll be going out with them tonight."

CHAPTER FOUR

I met Dylan in his room. Our relationship could best be described as hot and cold. When we first met, we couldn't keep our hands off each other. I wasn't attracted to him during full moons, for obvious reasons, but apart from that, he was my type. I've never been attracted to the Ken-doll types. I never once had a crush on anyone who sang in a boy band. I wasn't into especially rugged men, either. I liked nice-looking men who were more brain than brawn. A sense of humor was a plus. If a guy couldn't hold a decent conversation, I wasn't interested, no matter how chiseled his abs might be or how large a truck he might drive.

I might be a bit of an airhead at times, but I was always a good student. I was a bookish type, into role-playing games and computers. As such, I'd always had a lot of guy friends who were generally considered geekish. I had my limits. I wasn't into the disheveled, barely-ever-showered, lived-in-their-mother's-basement types. More than a fair share of guys like that had been in the computer programming classes and role-playing communities I used to frequent. They tended to have too many insecurities and mommy issues for my tastes. You might be surprised, though, how many nice-looking fellas were also geeks at heart. Dylan fit that profile. He wasn't the kind of guy that girls fawned over, but he was cute enough that most girls would give him a chance if he took the initiative. He had a kind face with dimples. His eyes were dark and alluring. He had an average-sized frame and had more tone to his body than his baggy clothes revealed.

Dylan was brave and confident, but not arrogant. A little confidence and a sense of humor went a lot farther with me than a handsome face and muscles.

Insecurity was a major turnoff for me. There are two kinds of insecure guys: those who are too shy to make a move or initiate a conversation, and those who are insecure but they cover it up with bravado and cockiness. The latter type usually came on to me when I visited the clubs in New Orleans. They usually bought me a drink and then acted like they were a prize, as if I should think I'd won the lottery when they flirted with me. Such boys might make good eating for a vampire, but I wasn't sure I had enough control to feed directly from the jugular and not go too far. Not without Dracula there to stop me if I went into a frenzy. Given that hunters were in the area, feeding directly was also ill-advised. Nine out of ten vampires whose existence ended at the sharp end of a hunter's stake met their fates within hours of a reckless feed.

Dylan was packing a duffel bag. Werewolves always needed a set of clothes nearby for the morning after. They each had stories about times they woke up naked, their clothes from the night before lost or ripped to shreds, and how they managed to sneak their way home while cupping their dangly bits and taking cover wherever they could.

"Dracula still obsessing over ghosts and ghouls?" Dylan asked.

I nodded. "Obsessed is an understatement. It's almost to the point that I'm worried he's overlooking threats we already know are out there. He wants to go look into patient records at the asylum tonight."

"He realizes it's a full moon, right?"

I nodded. "He told me to go and follow you around in the astral plane."

Dylan shook his head. "Those spirits in that place have been dead a while. You'd think they could wait three more days. Besides isn't breaking and entering more of your specialty?"

I laughed. "I only rob banks."

Dylan grinned. "Blood banks."

I nodded. "Yeah, well, they're still banks. Haven't had to do that in a while. Not since Dracula started buying bottles from Laveau's."

"That restaurant gives me the creeps."

"Because it caters to supernaturals?"

Dylan nodded. "Werewolves are different. Twenty-eight days out of the month, we're as normal as anyone. The two or three nights a month when we wolf out, we wouldn't be exactly welcome. That place might cater to supernaturals, but it isn't really for werewolves."

I nodded. "I can sort of relate. Before my vampirism came into full force, my brooch kept my supernatural side at bay most of the time. It took a while before I had any cravings, and at first, it was only when the sunlight invigorated my vampirism. Now, the brooch doesn't do much to tame my tummy. It's not good for much except going astral."

Dylan chuckled. "That's still a pretty handy ability. I wish I had one."

He had worn it before, when we were fighting Samuel and the Weird Sisters. "You can borrow it sometime if you need to," I offered.

Dylan shook his head. "I can't imagine why I'd have an urge to go invisible anytime soon. Besides, as cool as it was, it was also pretty terrifying. I was afraid I'd lose contact with the physical world and fly off into space at any moment."

"I suppose going astral makes us a lot like ghosts. When my

brooch is activated, I'm not strictly bound to the limits of the material world. So long as my mind recognizes walls, doors, the earth under my feet, it's as if they're real on the astral plane, too."

"Well, if it means anything, I'm every bit as confident with you watching my furry back as I'd be if Dracula was flying above."

I kissed Dylan on the cheek. "I appreciate you saying so."

Dylan's cheek rouged on contact. We were taking things slow. A vampire/werewolf romance wasn't entirely conventional. We also had to be careful. If he ever bit me, even in human form, I'd be sleeping beauty for a century. Kisses didn't have the same effect, thank God. Whatever contagion werewolves passed along that impacted vampires had to be introduced from the wolf's saliva directly into the bloodstream. What if I had a cut in my mouth and we kissed? So far I'd been lucky. Maybe a small wound like that wasn't enough to absorb the contagion. There wasn't any good way to test it out that didn't involve hundred-year-long consequences. While there wasn't any record of it happening, any other activity that included an exchange of fluids might have the same paralyzing effect. It was a good thing that we'd used protection in the past. Now that we knew the risk, though, we couldn't trust it. No form of protection is perfect.

Needless to say, our incompatible biologies made intimacy impossible. It was like pouring water over the spark we'd both *wanted* to develop into a raging inferno of passion. When the body is resisting what the heart wants, it's downright frustrating, if not infuriating. Dylan understood that we couldn't take things further. That didn't mean our feelings for each other just went away.

The only hope we had was that I'd become a master of the Scholomance like Dracula. The problem was that I'd already tried and the Scholomance rejected me. The path of light did, at least. I couldn't become a master of the path of light, because I'd fed on humans since becoming a daywalker. Dracula got through because, since I'd turned him into a daywalker and the Weird Sisters had exorcised his darkness, he'd only fed from bottles and blood bags. The only way I could become a master of the Scholomance was if I embraced the path of darkness. Was love worth selling one's soul into darkness? If I returned to the Scholomance and entered the dark path, how would it change me? Would Dylan love me if I embraced the dark side of the force?

Dracula's advice was simple. Move on. There are plenty of fish in the sea. I wasn't really into fish. I'd dated a few guys who kissed *like* fish before. I wasn't eager to jump back into that pond. The heart wants what the heart wants. Moving on was easier said than done.

It took all my strength to pull myself away from Dylan, but I left his room and headed for the cafeteria. We didn't keep our blood in the fridge. Who likes cold blood? Gross. We had a large warmer that maintained the bottles at a healthy ninety-eight point six. It still wasn't the same as drinking from the tap, but this was well-aged blood. The bottles represented a variety of vintages. I didn't notice much difference. My palate wasn't so refined. So long as it was blood and it was warm, it hit the spot. Then again, I would just as soon drink a concord wine from Mogen David as I would a well-aged French merlot. In fact, I preferred the sweeter wines.

Dracula called me a philistine. Whatever that meant.

He had a more refined palate. He usually poured his bottle into a glass, and he never filled it to the brim. He swirled it around and gazed at it before he took small sips, swishing the blood in his mouth before swallowing. He'd usually say something like, "Oh, this one has delightful notes of the Rhine," or some shit. Without reading the label on the bottle he could tell you where the blood came from and the donor's heritage. He'd remark on their health conditions, the donor's general mood when the blood was drawn, and a variety of other worthless details that were lost on me as I chugged straight from the bottle.

As such, given that I didn't appreciate the finer things, the bottles were marked with Post-its. Those that Dracula was saving for special occasions had notes like *"Don't you dare"* written on them. He got a little creative with them.

I grabbed one that was labeled with a note reading, *"This blood's for you."* So long as I was full on the bottled stuff, I could resist the urge to bite every warm-blooded human I might encounter when out and about. If I got a real hankering for the fresh stuff, a homeless man named Leeroy Jenkins lived in a park to the north and was always happy to let me take a sip in exchange for cash. He didn't give up the good stuff for cheap. Nothing short of a Benjamin Franklin did the trick. Thankfully, Dracula had more money than he could ever use and he didn't mind spreading the wealth.

Even so, I tried to avoid tapping Leeroy as much as possible. The more I drank fresh blood, the more I wanted it. Better to stick to the bottled shit and maintain a semblance of civility than find myself on a bender and, likely soon thereafter, facing off with a hunter.

I shoved my thumb into the cork, twisted my wrist, and popped the bottle open. It was a nice little trick Dracula taught me. It took a few tries to master, and more than once I'd crumbled the cork and had to filter the blood through cheesecloth before I drank it. Now, though, I had it down to an art.

I tipped the bottle back and chugged. What I really wanted was a keg. Our suppliers at Laveau's didn't offer that, though. They were as hoity-toity as Dracula.

I wiped my mouth and belched. I was that kind of lady. It hit the spot, and a surge of energy came over me. The school had a playground out back with most of the equipment gone. I could have run circles around it.

Instead, I changed my clothes. I was going astral for the night, mostly. I still needed to be prepared in case I had to get down and dirty with any hunters who might show up. Cargo pants. Hiking boots. A tank top. I slipped the long sheath for my silver sword through my belt loops and put the blade into it. Hopefully I wouldn't need it, but I was preparing for the worst.

I checked myself out in a full-length mirror that I'd added to my bedroom. The old classroom gave me more room than I knew what to do with. I had a chalkboard on the wall, too, and about a third of the alphabet was still stapled or glued to the wall above it. Dylan's pack, when it was significantly larger and before he was alpha, had used the schoolhouse as a den for more than a year. They'd cleaned up the place, but a werewolf den isn't known for being tidy or elegant. Dracula had big plans, though. Leave it to a count with Victorian tastes to come up with and pay for interior design.

I liked my look. I wouldn't say I was a tomboy, but I'd always admired tough girls. Until I met Zoey, I was anything but. Get yourself abducted by vampires and become one yourself, and you'll turn into a tough chick, too. Unless you're a dude, in which case it would take a lot more to become a tough chick. But who am I to tell you it's not possible? Let your inner diva soar.

I pinned my brooch onto my tank top. It was a fancy piece, shaped like a bird with a crystal in the middle. The styles clashed, but function was more important than fashion. We still had a few hours before nightfall, but when it came to werewolves and full moon prep, you couldn't start too soon. They usually arrived a few hours early, just in case they discovered people camping where they hoped to run wild for the night.

Dylan knocked on my door, and when I answered he looked me up and down. "Damn."

"I'm a redheaded GI Jane, right?"

Dylan laughed. "You're carrying a sword. I was thinking more like Xena Warrior Princess."

I grinned. "I'll take it."

Logan and Ian were waiting in the hall. Logan was what you'd call a ladies' man. He was such a flirt that he'd put Leon Phelps to shame. He was a tall, dark-haired, blue-eyed, male-model type, and a lot of girls reciprocated his flirtations. He never came on to me, though. Dylan was alpha, and Leon knew better than to try. Once a wolf "claims" a female, the others know to steer clear. No, Dylan didn't pee on me. I might be a bloodsucker, but I ain't that freaky. He may have imprinted on me somehow, the way the wolves did in *Twilight.* I wished he *could* imprint on me, in more ways than one, but that wasn't going to happen any time soon.

Ian was almost the exact opposite. He wasn't ugly, by any means, but he wasn't going to catch anyone's eye any time soon, either. He had plain features, was a little chubby, and had shoulders that sloped downward. I don't think he'd looked me in the eye once. He found females intimidating. It was funny, though, that when they shifted he was the more glamorous beast. He stood taller than the others when on all fours and had all the confidence that his human-self lacked. As I understood it, when the pack was larger and a few females had still been among them, he shifted into a canine playa under a full moon. It was a running joke that he'd never gotten any action that wasn't doggy style. Apparently, he and Lizzie, one of the werewolves who was killed in our fight with the Weird Sisters and the Van Helsing brothers, used to go at it like rabbits every full moon, and hardly said two words to one another the rest of the month. He was the only werewolf among them who enjoyed being a wolf more than being a human.

All three guys had large duffel bags hanging from their shoulders. This wasn't their first rodeo. It was the first time I'd gone out with them on a full moon, though and I was both excited and apprehensive about it. Since the Weird Sisters had compelled the pack to attack the French Quarter, hunters from all around the country were swarming the area every full moon.

How could one vampire chick thwart a team of hunters on a

werewolf hunt? The biggest advantage I had was that the hunters weren't looking for vampires. They were after wolves. If any of them ventured into the swamp, they'd never see me coming, and since they weren't on a vampire hunt, I hoped they wouldn't be prepared if I had to fight them off.

CHAPTER FIVE

We piled into the van Dracula had bought me before we moved from Kansas City to New Orleans—a Toyota Sienna. He bought the van because he thought it was cute to buy me a van that shared my name. It wasn't exactly my style. If it were up to me, I would have picked out something fast and loud, like a Camaro or a Mustang. I'd never had a classic muscle car, but when I was a girl, my best friend's father rebuilt them as a hobby. He'd said he'd build one for me when I was sixteen if I could pay his expenses. I got a job at Sonic to save up, but they moved away for a job when I was fifteen and I never got my dream car. Some dreams never die.

We drove out to as far a remote area as my soccer-mom van could go without getting stuck, about an hour out from New Orleans. I turned down a gravel road that had so many weeds growing out of the crest in the middle that I heard them brush against the underbelly of the van as I drove. The fact that there *was* a road meant people found reasons to go there. The condition of the road meant that it wasn't a lot of people and they didn't travel there often. It was in desperate need of more gravel and a good resurfacing. At least my van had all-wheel drive. If it rained and the road turned muddy, I wasn't sure I'd be able to get out.

Thankfully, my weather app indicated that a clear night was expected. The wolves were glad about that, too. They didn't have any choice but to be outside, and no one likes the smell of wet werewolf.

We still had about an hour and a half before sunset. Since the moon was full regardless of the sun's position in the sky, Dylan said that they could shift at any time twenty minutes before or after sunset. They needed to scout the area as well as possible while still in human shape. If anyone was in the area, we wouldn't have much time to find an alternate location. It was a little too close for comfort in my opinion, but what did I know? These wolves had shifted dozens of times before and knew their routine. I followed their lead and kept my distance. Once the shifts started, it would be obvious. It could take anywhere from one to five minutes for each wolf to complete his transformation. According to Dylan, a few factors like diet and mood could impact the ease or pain with which the transformation occurred. Usually, in a remote area without worry of hurting anyone, the shift was easier than when one was anxious or tried to mentally resist the shift.

I was glad I was in hiking boots. I could have gone astral straight away and skipped right over the mud and swampy waters, but it felt rude to up and disappear too soon.

We didn't find any evidence of anyone lurking nearby, but that didn't mean hunters weren't out there waiting. Unless they were amateurs, the hunters knew how to cover their tracks and lie low. The more experienced hunters knew ways to mask their scent so the werewolves wouldn't smell them in advance. I wasn't sure what they had to spread on their bodies to accomplish that, but it probably wasn't baby lotion. It had to be something native to the area, but also something with a strong enough odor to cover up the human scent. My best guess was alligator shit.

Whatever possessed someone to become a hunter was an enigma I'd never solve. Sort of like why people became proctologists. All those years in medical school to spend your life looking at people's buttholes? No, thank you! I'll get a day job and skip the student loans.

Hunters were almost as crazy. Sane people run away from vampires, werewolves, or any other monster that might be out there. To go into monster hunting, you have to have a screw loose somewhere.

The sun was past the horizon and a reddish-orange hue was illuminating the sky when it started happening.

Dylan, Logan, and Ian started undressing as the urge welled up within them. Dylan said that the sensation that signaled the change usually gave them less than a minute to prepare. It was a bummer. I had been looking forward to the show.

Instead, no sooner did they get off their shirts than their spines started expanding. Now, it was like watching three hunchbacks of Notre Dame remove their drawers. Not sexy. Not even a little.

The fur bursting from their skin didn't help. Seeing their bodies bend, expand, and change was grotesque. I also couldn't stop watching. It was repulsive and fascinating all at once.

I tapped my brooch. Dylan had warned me that the first few seconds after the change can be especially disorienting, and there was no telling how any of them might behave before they managed to get a semblance of wits about them.

It was best if I watched from the comfort of another plane of existence.

From what little I knew about the experience, a werewolf retained his human memories, but the change also had a profound impact on one's urges and personality. It was like any fears and mental barriers that one had as a human went away. That explained why a shy guy like Ian, who was a perv at heart like most guys, turned into a womanizer as a wolf. Okay, womanizer might not be the right word when it came to were-wolves, but bitchanizer doesn't have the same ring to it.

All three of them howled at the moon once it appeared in the sky. It probably wasn't smart given that hunters might have been out there, but some instincts are difficult to swallow. Dylan was more concerned with ensuring that they didn't start hunting down human hearts for a midnight snack than he was worried about a few howls or growls.

A breeze fluttered through the cypress branches above, and the wolves all turned toward the direction of the wind's origination to sniff the air. They picked up something and took off that way. I couldn't have kept up with them if I was in the material world—bottled blood was nothing like the real thing—but on the astral plane, I could move just as fast. I skimmed over the waters as the wolves bounced and splashed through the algae-covered swamp.

When this was over, even after they returned to human form, those boys were going to be *nasty.* I wish I'd thought to bring blankets to cover the seats.

They were having fun chasing each other around. I even caught Dylan chasing his own were-tail once. I filed that in the back of my mind as something I could raz him about later. It's one thing to chase tail. It's another thing when it's your own.

It looked like it was going to be a calm night. The wolves were cutting loose. I was relaxing. I didn't dare leave the astral plane just in case my presence triggered something with the wolves, but I was as comfortable as I could be given the fact that I was effectively wandering around the swamp like a ghost.

Bang!

A loud gunshot startled me out of complacency. The wolves scattered. It didn't look like any of them were hit. If this was a hunter who knew what he was doing, he was likely packing silver bullets. It didn't matter where a wolf was shot or stabbed with silver. A silver bullet to the heart or head would kill the werewolf instantly, but even a shot that wouldn't be mortal in most instances would fester and drop the wolf later, sometimes after they'd already returned to human form.

I couldn't let the hunter get off another shot. I ran in the direction the gunshot came from and found a man, alone, hiding in the brush. He was dressed in camouflage and held a gun. He was taking aim. I couldn't wait, so I pressed my brooch and yanked the gun from his hand.

I flashed my fangs. The man was wearing a headset.

"A fucking vampire!" he screamed.

I slammed the butt-end of his rifle into his head and knocked him out. He was talking to someone. That meant others were nearby, probably getting in position to shoot the wolves from another angle.

I pressed my brooch and took off like a flash of lightning across the swamp. The wolves were running away through the trees into denser foliage, probably into a trap.

I sped past the wolves and saw something move in the brush straight ahead. The barrel of a gun pointed out from the leaves.

He was aiming at Dylan. I moved between them and pressed my brooch just as the gunshot fired.

The silver bullet struck me in the shoulder. I couldn't be killed by a bullet, not even a silver one, but rage boiled up inside me. I charged the man in the brush and before I knew it I'd sunk my fangs into his neck.

His blood flooded my mouth. I gulped it down. With so much anger, I didn't hold back. Before I knew it, the man went limp, pale, and cold, and his blood stopped flowing into my mouth. I took a step back. My whole body was shaking.

"Holy shit," I whispered. "I just killed a man."

Dylan and the wolves saw what had happened, and they turned and ran back in the other direction. I wiped the blood from my mouth with my forearm and looked around. I could see in the dark better than humans, even better than werewolves, and now that I was full of human blood, my senses were turned up to the max. I heard every insect in the trees. I heard the wolves' paws strike the ground and their bodies splash through the swamp.

These were the only two hunters in the marsh. If there were more, I would have heard them breathing.

I gathered my wits. I needed to get back to the hunter I knocked out. I'd dropped his rifle somewhere in the swamp, but that didn't mean he didn't have other weapons on hand.

I ran back to where he was. He was just starting to come to, rubbing his brow. When he saw me, he gasped and tried to scurry away from me. I leaped on him and grabbed him by the neck.

"Who the hell are you and what are you doing here?"

"What do you think I'm doing? Why are you protecting were-wolves? Vampires don't like werewolves."

"It's none of your business."

"Help me!" the man screamed.

"No one will hear you. Your friend is dead."

"You bitch!"

"Want to join him, asshole?"

The man's lips quivered. "Please don't!"

"You're a hunter. Are you connected to the Van Helsings?"

"I'm not telling you shit!"

"Good. I don't want you to tell me shit. I want the truth."

"They'll kill you. All of you!"

"So you are in contact with the Van Helsings."

"You're the one who killed their brother. They said it was a redheaded vamp. She could walk in the sun."

I licked my lips. I knew at that moment I couldn't let the man leave. I had his friend's blood on my face and arm. If I let him go, now, he'd have a vendetta. He'd join the Van Helsings to come after me. Who was I kidding? They were coming after me eventually, anyway. The Van Helsing brothers were clever enough that when these hunters went missing, they'd track them here.

They'd figure out right away that it wasn't werewolves but a vampire who had killed them. They'd put two-and-two together. What other vampire was there, apart from Dracula, who was working with and protecting werewolves?

A thousand emotions overwhelmed my mind. I was pissed that these hunters were trying to kill my friends. The gunshot wound in my shoulder would heal, but now it hurt like hell. The taste of the other hunter's blood was still in my mouth, and I wanted more. I *needed* more.

Before I could stop myself, I bit the man. I drank as much as I could. It was like Thanksgiving dinner. I couldn't get any more in my stomach, but I kept sucking it in until I couldn't. Then in a fury, I snapped the man's neck.

I stumbled backward and turned to see the three wolves staring at me with wide eyes. They'd seen what happened. They knew what I did.

It wasn't the first time I'd killed. I'd sliced off one of the Van Helsing brothers' heads, but he came back again thanks to his immortality elixir. I smashed James's skull with my boot. He wasn't coming back ever. That was different, though. I didn't have a choice. Tonight, I could have stopped the hunters without killing them. I could have bound them up, brought them back to the schoolhouse, and let Dracula interrogate them. Instead, I fed. I killed. And I fucking enjoyed it. The pleasure I felt scared the hell out of me.

I clenched my fists and screamed into the night sky. The wolves whimpered. They could have stopped me. They could have come after me, bit me, and I'd have gone night-night for a hundred years. Instead, they kept their distance. Were they *afraid* of me now?

The night had hardly started, and we had hours before the wolves shifted back. I didn't know what else to do. I couldn't stand there facing the wolves for the rest of the night. When a werewolf is looking at you as if *you're* the monster, it's chilling.

I couldn't face them. Not yet. I touched my brooch and disappeared. I took off running through the swamp until I found a stump in the distance. I sat on it and reappeared. I lowered my face to my hands and wept. I was ashamed. But damn it if I couldn't think of anything other than the taste of blood.

CHAPTER SIX

I sat in silence for about half an hour before I pulled my phone from my pocket and called Zoey. It was the middle of the night, and not a good time to call, especially someone who was within weeks of having a baby. But I needed my friend and I was in a panic.

The phone rang several times and went to voice mail.

I hung up. A few seconds later my phone rang. Zoey was calling me back.

"Sienna, what's wrong?"

"I fucked up."

"What do you mean you fucked up?"

"I just killed two men. I fed and I couldn't stop."

My words were met with a good five seconds of silence. Finally, she said, "Tell me what happened."

I explained the situation. I wasn't sure how much sense I was making. I was all over the place. When I finished, Zoey laughed.

"You didn't *fuck up*, Sienna. You did what you had to do to protect your friends."

"I didn't have to kill them, Zoey. The worst part of it is that I *liked* it. I'm still craving blood. I want more!"

Zoey sighed. "How many vampires do you think feel *guilty* after they feed?"

I grunted. "I don't know. All the vampires I've met outside of Dracula are assholes."

Zoey laughed. "He was an asshole once too, you know. Now he's just an awkward goof."

"I'm scared, Zoey. I don't know if I can stop."

"Take a deep breath. I've seen you stand up to gods. You defeated the Weird Sisters. You stopped Sorina and Samuel Van Helsing from trying to take over the government. Even the president looks to you for guidance as he's managing his vampirism. Every time you've faced something terrifying, you've overcome whatever stood against you. This is no different."

"It is different. There's a monster inside me. I can feel it."

Zoey laughed. "There's a monster inside all of us. You face it the same way you face other monsters. You dig deep and stand against it."

I took a deep breath. "You're right. I'm sorry for waking you up."

"It's fine, Sienna. Call any time."

"How's it going with you? Ready to have that baby?"

"I'm more than ready. Kevin has the nursery ready. I'll send you pictures later. I'm just ready to not be pregnant anymore."

I grinned. "I'd say I can relate, but I've never been pregnant. Probably won't. I don't think vampires can get pregnant. Even if I could, it's not like I can sleep with Dylan."

"That must be hard."

I chuckled. "I wish. There's nothing *hard* about it at the moment."

Zoey giggled. "You're worse than most boys, you know that?"

"I'm happy for you. You're going to be an awesome mom."

"Thanks for saying so. I'm nervous about it. You'd think having the weight of the world on my shoulders more than once would prepare me for motherhood. It really doesn't."

"I get it. Just like having faced off with badass enemies more powerful than me was never as frightening as the devil within me. The more personal something is, the more the battle has to be fought within, the more it feels like you're in it alone."

"It's not true, though. I have Kevin to help me with our baby. You have friends, too. It might *feel* like you're facing this demon alone, but it's only like that if you refuse to let the people who love you help."

I nodded. "That's why I called you. I wish you were here. These Van Helsings are relentless. You'd think Dracula would be laser-focused on the brothers, but he's more afraid that Abraham is going to come back as a ghost. He has us investigating haunted locations. He's at an old asylum now stealing old patient files so we can learn how to deal with the spirits in the place."

"Seriously? He sent you out with the wolves alone so he could research dead people?"

I grunted. "Pretty much. He's obsessed. Once he got it in his head that Abraham Van Helsing might come after us to avenge his son, it's like he's been blind to the real threat."

"It wouldn't hurt to know. I'm not getting around much, but I could easily forge a portal. I could go get Morty and he could take you back to the Scholomance. Maybe you could speak to Abraham and find out what his intentions really are."

I bit my lip. "I'm not sure Dracula would be on board with that. Walking right into Abraham Van Helsing's domain and confronting him would be like walking into a lion's den to find out if they really had a taste for flesh."

"Not necessarily. That's only true if he really is intent on exacting vengeance. If he isn't, well, then you can convince Dracula to refocus his priorities. Not to mention, it'll give you a little time for your cravings to settle. If you aren't in the company of flesh-and-blood humans for a while, you might be able to come back with more control over your cravings."

"I don't know. If Abraham is pissed and he sees me, I'm not sure I could take him."

"If you're going to the Scholomance through the void, there's not much he can do to you. Is Euryale still with Athena in Hades?

"She is."

"Then no matter what he does, all the gorgon has to do is bring you back again. He can't kill you in the void. What's the worst that could happen?"

I took a deep breath. "I suppose you have a point."

"I'll go see Morty in the morning. I'll call you if there's any problem. Otherwise, he'll come and get you tomorrow."

I nodded. "Well, he is the Grim Reaper. He might be busy."

"I know my brother. You're a dear friend to both of us. He'll find the time to help."

"Thanks, Zoey. Sorry again for waking you. Get your sleep. You have a big day coming up."

"I'll be sure to let you know when the baby is coming!"

"Do you know if it's a boy or a girl yet?"

"Kevin wanted it to be a surprise. That means if you send any gifts, make sure they're yellow or green. No pink or blue."

"Girls can wear blue. Boys can wear pink. It's the twenty-first century, Zoey."

Zoey laughed. "Well, you know Kevin. He's a traditionalist."

I smiled. "I'll just wait to send any gifts after the baby comes. I have your baby registry."

"Sounds good to me. Take care, Sienna. Remember. You've got this. Being a vampire, or a human, doesn't make you more or less of a monster. It's your choices that make the difference."

I said goodbye and hung up the phone. I still had a longing for more blood, but Zoey was right. Talking to her always calmed me down. Getting away for a while would help. It also wouldn't hurt if I could come back with good news—that Abraham Van Helsing didn't have any plans to haunt us. Perhaps Dracula was right, but finding out for sure would solve a lot of problems.

CHAPTER SEVEN

I sat on that tree stump for hours. I tried to close my eyes and meditate. I heard Dracula in my mind telling me to breathe deeply. To focus my mind on the sound of my breaths. It didn't work. My mind was still swarming with extrasensory inputs. It wasn't an overwhelming sense so much as an awareness. It was like feeding had awakened my inner predator.

I unsheathed my sword and swung it through the air. It was either that or play one of those damned bubble-popping games on my phone for hours. I hoped that since meditation didn't work well for me, a little physical exertion might.

When all else fails, swing a sword at shit. You'll feel better. Just make sure the area is free of small children and pets. I sliced my blade through bushes and bramble. Something large swam through the water in the opposite direction. Probably an alligator. I scared a freaking *gator* away. I wasn't sure if it made me a badass bitch, or such a vile monster that even large reptiles fled when I was on the scene. Maybe some of both. Zoey was right. I had been protecting my friends. I let my rage get a foothold, though. Hunters aren't necessarily bad humans. They aren't generally villains. They're just a bit closed-minded when it comes to judging creatures they don't understand. They tend to generalize and color all of us with the same crayon. Most of them did what they did because they felt they were protecting people. Some of them became hunters because they'd lost people they loved to something supernatural. We weren't that different. I fought monsters, too. It just so happened that I became one in the process.

I had to do better. I couldn't let my rage take over again. With blood in my system already from the bottles I downed back at the schoolhouse, I should have remembered that my senses were heightened, and that didn't just apply to the usual five senses. It was also true of my emotions. After I fed on those hunters, I understood why a lot of vampires went on feeding frenzy benders. People were like Pringles. Once you popped, you couldn't stop.

My saving grace at the moment was the relief I got from talking to my best friend and the fact that I was in a godforsaken swamp with no one edible in the vicinity. The time I had to wait for the wolves gave me the time to come down off my blood high.

Little by little, my senses returned to normal. Along with the fading sensations, my guilt also waned. I was still troubled by what happened, but the panic was gone.

What I wasn't looking forward to was the awkward drive home. After the way the wolves were looking at me when I killed that hunter, I didn't know how they'd respond back in human form.

When the sun started to rise, I went astral, not because I needed to but because it was a lot easier to get through the swamp that way.

Dylan, Logan, and Ian were all standing in front of my van stark naked. When they saw me, they turned to hide their preciouses.

I snickered, reached into my pocket, retrieved my fob, and unlocked the van. "Sorry, guys."

I turned to give them a little privacy as they retrieved their duffle bags and got dressed.

After they were dressed, I got in the driver's seat and pressed the ignition button. This fancy hybrid was so quiet that when it started, the only way I knew it was running was the green "Ready" light on the dash.

No one said a word as I pulled back onto the gravel road and drove back toward the highway.

Dylan broke the silence. "I think I speak for all of us when I say, 'thank you.'"

I tilted my head. "Thank you? That's not what I was expecting. You saw what I did."

"I did," Dylan reached over from the passenger seat and rested his hand on my leg. "You saved our lives. If you weren't there, those hunters would have picked us off one by one. You took a bullet for me, Sienna."

I rubbed my shoulder with one hand while I held the wheel steady with the other. "It was nothing. Bullet went all the way through. Hurts like a bitch, but I'll live. By tomorrow, I'll be back to normal."

"It wasn't nothing," Logan piped up. "It was badass!"

"I drank that man dry," I reminded him. "How is that badass?"

I glanced at Logan in the rearview mirror. He shrugged. "It was for the best. If you didn't kill those men, they'd just regroup and come for us again tomorrow night."

I sighed. I'd been so anxious about everything that it had skipped my mind that we were going to have to do this *again*. "You should still find another place before tomorrow. If those hunters tracked you to this swamp, there's a good chance other hunters knew about it as well."

Dylan looked at me. I could barely see his grin out of the corner of my eye. "We'll figure it out. We may want to find some-place a little more remote."

"More remote than this?"

"Further from the city, I mean. The hunters are all over New Orleans. Ever since the incident on Bourbon Street. The further away we go, the less likely it is any will track us there."

"How did they track us here?" Ian asked. "We didn't tell anyone where we were going."

"It may have been random," I guessed. "There were only two hunters. If they knew for sure which swamp you were going to, they'd probably have brought more. Those hunters knew the Van Helsing brothers. They'd surely be with them if they knew for sure that's where you'd be."

Dylan nodded. "We still need another place. If anything, when those hunters don't show up and report to whatever other hunters they're in league with, especially the Van Helsings, they'll figure out that this was the swamp where we were."

I nodded. "And when the other hunters come looking for them, they'll find the bodies. They'll know it was a vampire kill. Wolves don't drain people like that."

Dylan turned and stared out his window. "That means they'll go out more prepared to deal with a vampire tomorrow night."

"Most likely," I agreed. "If they find the bodies in time. Knowing the efficiency of the Van Helsings, and the hunters they might be working with, I'd bet they will."

Dylan looked back at me. "Are you okay?"

I nodded. "I will be. I'm still a little bit shocked by what I did. I never drained a man like that before."

"You feel guilty?"

"A little. Okay, a lot. But I'm managing. At first, the rush, the sensations I felt after drinking that much blood, it was like I was an addict who couldn't get enough. If there was anyone else in that swamp, any humans, I don't know that I could have held back."

"How are you feeling now?"

I bit my lip. "Better. Most of those urges subsided after a few hours. It still scared me to lose control like that."

"Well, it's a good thing it happened there where the only people you could hurt were those hunters. At least now you know what it's like. You'll be better prepared if anything ever happens like that where there are more people around."

"That's a good point. I hadn't thought about it like that."

"I'm just saying it could have been worse. You learned something about yourself and the damage that resulted was minimal."

"I still killed two men," I insisted.

"Who would have killed us," Logan shot back. "One way or another, it was going to be us or them. If you didn't kill them, we'd either be dead or we would have killed them ourselves."

I pressed my lips together and rubbed my eyes. With the morning sun shining through the windshield, an extra strength came over me. Vampires are *all* strong. Until a few months ago, I was vulnerable at night. I was like any human. Little did I know that the vampirism within me was growing stronger and that it was just a matter of time before whatever semblance of humanity I enjoyed in darkness would give way to my *other* nature. I was still stronger during the day. I was faster, too.

The real blessing in being a daywalker, though, was that I lacked the photosensitivity that plagued most of my kind. While other vampires were hiding away and lurking in the shadows, I could go anywhere I wanted. I could even go tanning on the beach. Not that my skin *would* tan. Technically, a tan is the result of damage to the skin. Since we vamps heal quickly, not even a daywalker could tan. But I wouldn't sunburn either, so there was that. I could still enjoy the warmth of the sun beaming down upon my skin. I also had access to stores and businesses that closed before dark. You'd be surprised how many vampires you might find at the 24-hour Walmart in the middle of the night. And you thought you'd seen strange people there during the day.

The sunlight also had a calming effect on my mind. It gave me a clarity of thought that I lacked at night. I don't know if it made me any smarter, but it was like my mind worked faster. I saw things as obvious that might have befuddled me in darkness.

Zoey was right. I needed to go back to the Scholomance and confront Abraham. I needed to know what we were dealing with before nightfall. If hunters found us once, they'd find us again. Now that two hunters were dead, they'd be out for blood. I needed to put this ghost business to rest and get Dracula on board. It was the *living* Van Helsings—all the hunters who joined them in their monster-slaying line of work—who were the immediate threat.

CHAPTER EIGHT

"How was your night?" Dracula didn't raise his eyes from his desk when I stepped into his room. He was poring over stolen medical records he must've located at the asylum while I was out fighting and feasting upon hunters.

"There were two hunters out there. I took care of it."

"Look at this. One of the doctors was involved in experimental treatments. He'd insert a rod into the brain through the eye socket and send electrical pulses into the brain. He was trying to combine electro-shock therapy with lobotomies."

I gulped. "That's horrifying."

Dracula nodded. "His theory was that mental illness was caused by an interruption in the electric impulses that flow through the brain. He thought an extra jolt could jump-start the brain and get it working again."

"He got away with that shit?"

"So far as I can tell. For a while, at least. Check this out." Dracula grabbed another page he'd pulled from the files at the asylum. It was a copy of an article about a riot at the asylum.

I skimmed the first couple of paragraphs. "The patients murdered the doctor in his office."

"It's no wonder those spirits are so restless," Dracula mused. "Many of them died at the hands of Doctor Quentin Feuerhahn, then some of his patients killed him. I suspect he continues to torment the patients trapped there in death."

"We can't know that for sure," I pointed out.

"It's a reasonable deduction."

"Maybe," I admitted before I moved on to what I really wanted to talk about. "Look, Drac. I bit those hunters. I drained one of them dry. I would have drained the other one if I wasn't full."

Dracula frowned and finally looked up at me. "How do you feel now?"

I shrugged. "Mostly normal."

"That's good. The first time that happened to me, the craving consumed me for a week. I wasted an entire village in less than a week. That you're doing so well now is encouraging. I imagine that starting off on bottled blood for so long allowed your body to adapt gradually. In the old days, most vampires didn't have the benefit of stored blood."

"You're not angry?"

"How could I, of all people, judge you, Sienna? It was expected. If the only people who died are the hunters who wanted to kill you anyway, well, I'd say that they got what was coming to them."

"Maybe. But those hunters knew the Van Helsing brothers. Once they figure out I killed two of them, they'll be pissed. We need to work together to help protect the wolves tonight."

Dracula grabbed a ball-point pen from the table and clicked it open and closed. "Dylan is the alpha. He'll come up with a plan. If they need our help, all they have to do is ask."

I stared at Dracula blankly for a few seconds, but he didn't notice. He was absorbed again in the patient files.

I shook my head and returned to my room. It wasn't so much that Dracula was being callous. It wasn't that he wasn't willing to help the wolves. He just didn't think the hunters were as great a threat as they were. Maybe he figured the Van Helsing boys weren't as formidable as their father. Perhaps he'd faced so many hunters through the years that this was just another day at the office. I needed to pull his head out of his pale ass.

What Dracula didn't understand was that all the time he was earning his master's in the path of light in the Scholomance, I spent what felt like damn near a year hanging out with Abraham Van Helsing. We played a lot of Monopoly. We shot the shit. We developed a relationship, and I wasn't afraid of him. If I could just talk to him, and clear the air over what happened, I thought he'd understand. If he knew what his sons were up to, I couldn't believe he'd agree with their agenda.

I got a change of clothes and a towel from my room then hit the showers in what used to be the girls' locker room. I still had dried blood on my arm. I wasn't as dirty or smelly as the wolves, mostly because I avoided the worst of it by going astral, but I still needed to clean up.

After I showered and dressed, I returned to my room. I was startled when I saw Morty there sitting on the edge of my bed. I knew he was coming, I just didn't expect him there at that very moment.

"Hey, Morty. I take it Zoey got ahold of you?"

Morty nodded. "Ready to go?"

I sighed. "I guess so. I need to be back by tonight."

Morty nodded. "Not a problem. It just so happened that Athena and Euryale were in the underworld for our weekly meeting."

"They come to your office for meetings?"

"It's standard protocol. We compare our records to ensure all the souls on the reaper schedules reached their eternal destinations. It's not common, but we've had a few spirits who managed to escape during the handoffs through the years."

"The handoff to the boatman?"

"And his handoff of the souls to perdition. It only happens on occasion, but when a wandering spirit gets loose, we need to know about it."

"What's the worst that could happen? A ghost living in the underworld with reapers doesn't sound like a problem."

Morty shook his head. "You wouldn't think so. But spirits who have the strength to escape during the handoff are often also capable of possession."

I raised an eyebrow. "Ghosts can possess people?"

Morty nodded. "And reapers. Usually, they're pissed, too. Believe it or not, a lot of dead folk aren't exactly fond of reapers."

I chuckled. "Gee, I wonder why not."

"They shouldn't be. We make sure they get where they're supposed to go."

"And if that destination is hell, I doubt they're especially grateful for that."

"I suppose they aren't. Believe it or not, though, hell is preferable to wandering as a spirit. Ghosts tend to get a little wonky over time. Year after year, seeing everything that's going on, but struggling to manifest or communicate in any way, is enough to drive anyone crazy. Hell might not be pleasant, but especially under Athena, it's not nearly the level of torment that most spirits endure if they're stuck where they don't belong."

I pressed my lips together. "You can't really blame them. If I knew I was being ferried to hell, I'd probably fight like hell, too. I'd stow away with the boatman and look for my first chance to disembark in heaven, instead."

Morty shook his head. "That's the worst thing that could happen. A spirit that's marked for hell would only bring chaos into heaven if he ever made it there. A damned spirit in heaven is like an infection. It screws with everyone's personal paradise. It throws everything out of balance."

I shook my head. "I'm not going to pretend to understand how that's possible, but it doesn't sound good."

"It isn't. Anyway, as I was saying, Athena and Euryale were already in town. They're waiting in my office. Lucky you, you won't have to pass through hell to reach them this time."

I chuckled. "I'll take good luck wherever I can find it."

Morty formed a portal to the underworld. He allowed me to pass through first. I landed in his office and he showed up right behind me.

"Sienna!" Euryale ran to me and hugged me. We had been roommates for a while back in Kansas City when she and her other gorgon sister were staying with Zoey and me. After that, they'd moved into the apartment next to ours.

I hugged her back. Her snake hair was covered with a shawl, per usual. "Good to see you, Euryale."

Athena, the goddess and recently coronated queen of hell, had a blank look on her face. She and I weren't friends. There was a time when we were enemies. She stepped up to me and got straight to business. "Morty tells me you wish to return to the Scholomance."

I nodded. "I need to clear the air with Abraham Van Helsing. I shouldn't be long. I need to make sure I'm out of there before nightfall."

"You know how to return on your own," Athena reminded me.

"Right. But you know how wonky time is there. If it's taking too long, for whatever reason, I'll need Euryale to bring me back."

Euryale nodded. "That won't be a problem."

"There's something you should know," Athena added. "For whatever reason, I haven't been able to access the Scholomance for the last couple months."

I tilted my head. "I thought as the acting devil, you were in charge of the school."

Athena nodded. "I thought so, too. There's only one force that could prevent me from accessing the place. That's if the old devil has somehow escaped his prison in the void and taken refuge in the Scholomance."

My eyes widened. "Hades is *in* the Scholomance?"

"I can't confirm it. But he founded the place. If anyone knows a way to lock me out of the Scholomance, it's him."

"If you can't get in, are you sure I can?"

Athena nodded. "You already passed the initial trials. I don't think Hades could lock you out. Your soul already has an imprint upon it that's like a universal key."

"Can I open the door and bring you with me?"

Athena shook her head. "It doesn't work that way. Do what you need to do. If you have the time, however, I need you to investigate exactly what's going on. If Hades has reclaimed his position as the headmaster of the Scholomance, there's no telling what he might be up to."

I nodded. "I'll see what I can find out. Are you sure it's safe for me to go there?"

Athena nodded. "Not even a god can destroy or harm a soul that's apart from the body. We'll make sure your body is safe here in stone until you return."

I took a deep breath. I wasn't exactly thrilled about encountering Hades. The few times I'd met him, he was an ass. He was the acting devil, the king of hell, for thousands of years, so I supposed it made sense. His line of work didn't exactly encourage mutual respect and positive self-talk.

"I'm ready."

"We'll be here waiting for you when you get back," Athena promised. "If you can figure out how or why he's keeping me out, or better, shut it down, I'll know. I just need a second and I can come in and help lock Hades back in his prison."

Euryale removed the shawl from her head to reveal the snakes slithering around vigorously atop her scalp. I only saw them for a half-second before my body seized up, and the next thing I knew I was back in the void. Sometimes, when Athena sent me there, I went straight to the Scholomance. Other times, I had to make my way there myself. I knew how the void worked. If I was looking for something, I'd find it. All I had to do was move through the darkness with my intentions front and center in my mind.

I stepped forward and the darkness morphed into a range of colors. I'd walked right into the Scholomance, the same room where I'd stayed with Abraham while Dracula was mastering the path of light.

Abraham's table was there. A game of Monopoly was set up, with fake money tucked under the board on two sides. The thimble was resting on Park Place and the horseman was in jail.

"Abraham," I called out. "Are you here?"

My voice echoed through the stone halls. I left the main room and followed the hallway that split in two directions—one toward the part of the Scholomance that catered to the path of light, the other to darkness.

I followed the hall of light, and it led to a dead-end. It was the wall that opened if you were permitted to enter the path toward mastering the path of light. When I went there before, it rejected me. Now that I'd fed and drained a man, the wall would never open for me.

Abraham wasn't there. Neither was Samuel.

My stomach turned. If he wasn't here, perhaps Dracula was right. Had he returned to Earth as a spirit to exact vengeance upon us for killing one of his sons? Was Samuel with him? Samuel wasn't a ghost. He still had a body.

I didn't see any sign of Hades, either. Perhaps Athena was wrong. What else could possibly explain her inability to access the Scholomance? I had to keep looking. The other hallway, the one that led to the path of darkness, was the only place left Abraham, Samuel, or Hades could be.

Samuel might have entered the trials, with Abraham to guide him and accompany him on the path. If they were beyond the wall, engaging the trials, I wouldn't know unless I stayed until they returned. If I had to, I'd wait as long as I could to find out for sure. There was no sense in that, though, if they were in the halls leading to darkness.

I walked back to where the hallways split. I continued down the hall toward the path of darkness. It wasn't that different from the hall leading to light. It was its opposite, a mirror image, just like Dracula described the relationship between the two paths.

The only difference was that as I moved down this hall, something tugged at me like a magnet attracting a piece of metal.

I stopped in my tracks. Perhaps this wasn't the best idea. I turned but I couldn't move. I couldn't leave the hall.

What the hell?

The pull on my body intensified, and the next thing I knew, I had left my feet and was floating down the hall. I couldn't fight it. I couldn't resist.

I reached a wall at the end of the hall, and a red energy swirled around the stone, creating a portal. It was like a vacuum. The portal sucked me right in.

I found myself in a dark room. When my feet hit the floor, a series of torches all around lit and illuminated walls formed of stone, black like onyx.

I turned and pressed my hands against the wall I'd passed through, but it wouldn't budge.

Welcome, Sienna. You've proven yourself worthy to begin the path toward a master of darkness.

The voice was deep, almost like that guy who did the narration for movie previews.

"I didn't choose this!" I screamed.

But you've been chosen, nonetheless.

"Who are you?" I demanded.

I am the darkness. I am what was before there was light.

I gulped. "You're not seriously going biblical on me, are you?"

The voice didn't respond right away. I waited almost a minute in silence before the darkness spoke again.

I am formless and void. I am the force that can be molded by the hands of a master. I am a power older than creation itself. The primal force.

"What if I don't want it?"

There is only one way to leave this place. You can return to the world as a master of darkness, or you can remain here forever.

I remembered what Dracula told me before, how I could leave the Scholomance and the void and return to my body. I had to focus on something that connected me to my body, to genuine joy and happiness. I had to seek it with my whole spirit. The only thing I could think about was the taste of the hunter's blood. How it invigorated my body and awakened my senses. I closed my eyes and focused. I thought about Dylan. I recalled my adventures with Zoey. No sooner did those images come to mind than my thoughts immediately returned to blood.

I opened my eyes. I wasn't back in Morty's office. I wasn't in my body.

I was standing in a cave. A single fire burned in the middle of the chamber. Strange sigils were written in blood on the walls all around me.

"Where the hell am I?"

You are on the path of the first.

"The first what?"

The first vampire. The first master of the Scholomance.

I tried to swallow, but my mouth was dry. My throat seized. I turned.

A woman with long white hair and eyes black like coal stood before me. She was naked and her body was covered in blood.

"My child of night!" The woman cackled. She extended her arm toward me. "Take and drink, that you might be reborn as a master of darkness."

I clenched my fists. My mind screamed at me to run away, but I couldn't. A surge of energy overwhelmed me and my senses expanded, just as they had when I'd fed on the hunter. I could hear the woman's heart beating in her chest. It drew me in.

I sank my fangs into her wrist and her blood flowed into my mouth.

"Yes! Drink and don't stop!"

Her words echoed in my mind. I didn't stop. I couldn't. All I could do was swallow her blood. It didn't taste like the hunter's blood. It tingled and numbed my mouth and throat. I pulled away. My vision blurred. I saw two, then three, images of the woman before I fell to my knees and collapsed on the floor.

CHAPTER NINE

When I opened my eyes, I was hundreds of feet over a desert. A warm air passed over me. I screamed but something more like a screech came out of my mouth. I flailed my arms and felt them catch the wind, and when I looked to my right, my arm wasn't just an arm. It was a wing. The other arm matched. My fingers were a part of the wing. I was a bat.

When Dracula was a master of the dark path in the Scholomance, he could turn into a bat. He could also turn into a black dog. If that was the case, maybe I could run with the wolves. I'd be the runt of the litter, but hell, why not? A part of me was freaking out about all of this. I didn't want to follow the path of darkness. But if I was a *master* of the Scholomance, I could resist the werewolf's contagion. Dylan and I might have a shot.

I knew it was selfish to think about that given the greater concern that, by embracing the dark path, my more monstrous nature might take a greater hold on me. I didn't know what was happening. When the darkness spoke, he had referred to himself as a primal force, a magic of a kind that has existed since before the world came into being. I also remembered Zoey's words.

What I was didn't make me good or evil. It was my choices that mattered.

The darkness told me otherwise. What was happening right now wasn't my choice. I'd come to the Scholomance looking for Abraham Van Helsing. I wasn't looking for power or anything pertaining to the dark path. Where was Abraham? Where was Samuel? I'd tried to return to my body, but it didn't work. Was that my fault? Did I lack the focus to pull it off? Or was the darkness holding me here, forcing me upon a path I'd never intended to take?

I flapped my wings and experimented with flapping one side harder than the other, twisting my body, expanding my wings, and allowing the wind to carry me. I didn't know how I'd taken this shape, and worse, I didn't know how to change back.

I looked all around. Sand as far as the eye could see. The sun beat down on me. My daywalker advantages were still intact, and the light made me stronger by the second. Ironic, I suppose, that while the darkness welled up within me the light invigorated me from without.

In the distance, I spotted dozens of bodies swarming around like ants in an ant farm. A pillar of smoke rose into the sky beyond them.

As I flew closer, a familiar scent filled the air. Everyone knew that bats had a good sense of hearing, and if my condition meant anything, the phrase "blind as a bat" was inaccurate. I could see clearly. My sense of smell was also keen and, as a vampire bat, the fragrance of blood drew me in.

It was a small village. Several huts were ablaze. A band of raiders in long cloaks and scarves, carrying straight broadswords, were rounding up the villagers. They had several women with rings hooked through their noses linked together by a chain. The bloodied bodies of dozens of men were littered around the huts.

The scent was overwhelming. My little bat tummy gurgled. I couldn't take my eyes off those poor women and children, all in tears, their faces covered in blood from the rings that had been forced through their noses.

It wasn't their blood that harnessed my attention. It was their plight.

"What will it be? So much blood. Will you feast or will you fight?"

The darkness's question presented the dilemma. It wasn't a choice. I didn't have my sword. Would my brooch work? Was this real or just a vision created by the magic of the Scholomance, to determine the course my path into the darkness would take? I'd assumed that there was only one dark path, but now it appeared I still had a choice. Within the darkness, would I entertain my vampiric urges or would I embrace whatever humanity remained within me? Would I save these people, those who still survived, or take advantage of the chance to feed on their fallen?

It didn't have to be that way. These bandits were human. They had blood too, and if I bit them, they'd damn well deserve it. With a little blood and the sunlight fueling my strength, I'd be a force. The bandits wouldn't know how to kill me. They were wielding swords, not stakes.

I dive-bombed into the middle of the village, and as I thought about taking my usual shape again, my body expanded. I touched the brooch on my chest and went astral. My body wasn't even *in* the Scholomance. It was back in Morty's office. I wasn't sure that this was my real body, which meant the brooch I was wearing might have only been an illusion. If this was a vision created by the darkness, the vision had my usual abilities built in, including the enchantment that empowered my brooch.

I darted through the astral plane and found one of the bandits. I thrust my fist into his chest before I touched my brooch to rematerialize and yank the man's heart out through his ribs. I took a bite out of it, swallowed the blood, and spit out the flesh.

As the bandit fell, I grabbed his sword. With my body flowing with power from the sun and the man's blood, I swung it with a fury at the bandits.

They closed in around me once they realized what was happening, but they couldn't take me down. A swift kick sent one of the bandits flying back and crashing into a burning hut. The flames caught his cloak. I swung the sword in a circle and sliced through three abdomens at once.

A blade struck me in the back. I stood and turned to the man who hit me. "That's what I call a cheap shot, asshole."

I reached around and grabbed the blade that was stuck in my back and pulled it out. I was a double-sword-wielding badass now. The bandits spread out. They were cursing, or maybe praying. I didn't know many gods who'd answer the prayers of murderous thieves raiding an innocent village.

I chased them down, one by one. I was fast. I was automatic. I was *slaughtermatic*. I was bitch lightning. By the time I finished, there wasn't a single bandit left.

I used my vampiric strength to break the rings that held the prisoners together. They were in shock. I couldn't tell if they were more afraid of me or grateful I'd freed them. More than that, they were torn to the heart. Their men had been slaughtered before I arrived. Bodies were everywhere. The fragrance of their blood swirled with sand in the wind.

A single hut in the middle of the village was untouched by the flames. It didn't look like the other huts. It was barely touched by sand, and it was a crimson color that stood out from everything else that matched the tan hue of the sand.

Something inside me told me to check it out, so I stepped through a hide that covered the entrance to the hut. The same witch I'd seen before was sitting in front of a giant cauldron. Whatever she was brewing bubbled with a red energy that sparked through it.

"Who are you?" I demanded. "What the hell is happening?"

The witch smiled widely. Her teeth were yellow and crooked. "I am your creator."

I snorted. "What does that mean?"

"I made the first vampire. What you know as the Scholomance, founded in Romania, was founded based on magic and teachings of the priestesses under my tutelage in Ur, more than five hundred years before the Common Era. My name is Ennigaldi. I am the wife of the moon god, Sin."

"You're married to Sin? And you're a goddess?"

"Sin is merely the name of a god once revered by the Babylonians, Akkadians, and Assyrians. It is he who has spoken to you as the darkness. There is no connection between Sin and the notion of disobedience common in the Hebrew religion."

"Are you a god?" I pressed.

Ennigaldi chuckled. "I was born a human. I was Sin's human wife. For centuries, I've slumbered, waiting for the one who might carry the image of Sin. One of my children who might not only walk in the darkness but also in the light. When another appeared in the Scholomance, we thought we'd found our moon child."

"You're talking about Samuel Van Helsing?"

Ennigaldi nodded. "Like you, he is a vampire who can walk in the light. He was given the same test when we welcomed him on the path. He made a different choice. He did not save the women, but slaughtered everyone. He fed on their blood and proved himself unworthy to bear the mark of Sin."

I shook my head. "I felt the same urge. There was so much blood."

"But you resisted. My husband is darkness, but he is the god of the moon. The moon is also the light of the night. It reflects the sun into the darkness. It unites the paths of darkness and light. You are the one we've waited for, the one who might lead my children as the guardians of the moon, the creatures of the night who I once created that they might stand against the true creatures of darkness."

I snorted. "What creatures of darkness?"

"The children of the devil, the ones who took the lessons I taught in Ur and manipulated them to lead my children into villainy."

I nodded. "Like Dracula. He was once a master of the Scholomance in the path of darkness."

"He embraced the perverted magic that the devil you know as Hades once spread. He turned my warriors of the moon into children more like his demons. They are the true enemy, the creatures of darkness who know no light."

This was a lot to take in. "What happened to Samuel? Where is his father, Abraham Van Helsing?"

"When he failed the test, he was cast from the Scholomance. His father left with him."

I took a deep breath. "They're on Earth?"

Ennigaldi shrugged. "All I can say is that they are no longer here. Samuel left as a master of the Scholomance, one like Dracula before him who embraced the ways of Hades. You must stop him."

"Isn't Abraham a master of the path of light?"

"The path of light was created when Hades established the Scholomance, not that he would lead anyone on that path, but because it was the only way to separate the light of the moon from the darkness."

I cleared my throat. "When Dracula came here and mastered the path of light, he was a daywalker already."

"Indeed. To unite the paths, a herald of both paths must emerge. We believed, when Samuel arrived, it was he and his father who would bring these paths together. We were wrong. It was you and Dracula all along."

Every answer she gave raised more questions. "Why was I taken on this path? Was it because I'd killed a man?"

"It was necessary. These were the qualifications for entry to the mastery of the Scholomance dictated by Hades. We could not rewrite those rules. We had to work within the magic of the path and hope you might redeem yourself through the test. You did well, Sienna. There are not many who could do what you accomplished."

I pressed my lips together. "Are you the reason why Athena can't get into the Scholomance?"

"It is my husband. As a god within the void, he entered the Scholomance when the Van Helsing boy arrived. Athena is not Hades, but she's assuming his role. We could not allow another Greek god to stand in the way of our attempt to reunite the paths."

"What happens next? What am I supposed to do?"

"So long as a master of the dark path lives, the path of the moon cannot be realized. The darkness and light cannot be truly reunited."

"I need to stake Samuel Van Helsing."

The priestess-witch nodded. "That's one way to do it. You know the ways a vampire might be killed."

"Then what? You basically want me to moon the world, right?"

Ennigaldi laughed. "That's a colorful way to put it. The true creatures of darkness remain a threat. You must resume your places as my warriors, the children I made to protect the world from the children of Hades."

"The demons aren't a problem. Athena rules hell."

"She might rule it, but she is not their mother. Do not mistake her authority for control. Were the demons to leave hell, they would be beyond her reach."

I thought for a minute. "One question. If you made us, why the craving for blood? It doesn't do much to encourage us to be well-rounded contributors to society, much less an army against the forces of evil."

"Blood is life. It is also power. There are many forms of power that might be sought after in the world. Throughout history, no power has proven to be more potent than that which lies latent in blood. Blood sacrifices have long been used to pacify the gods. It can restrain the wrath of a vengeful deity. Not because a god desires blood, but because even the gods must bend to the power released in sacrifice. For most, blood simply sustains life. Life, after all, is a fantastic spell. A marvel of its own. There is more power within blood, however, than the generation of life. The vampire was made to realize the full potential of what already flows through human veins. To become humanity's greatest protector, even if the very power that vampires gain might make them humanity's greatest threat."

I snorted. "Quite a gamble, don't you think? Doesn't look like it's panned out so well to date. Most vampires I've met are monsters."

"Nothing worthwhile comes without risk. Humanity is fragile already. With or without the vampire, humans are already the agents of their own destruction. Add to that the children of Hades, the demons and devils, the monsters born out of his wrath, and it is a wonder that humanity has endured as long as it has."

"So vampires were supposed to be the agents of this moon god you married? That's what you're telling me?"

Ennigaldi grabbed a ladle and dipped it into her cauldron. She stirred it gently. "Most gods work through agents. Some deities create what you'd call angels. Others, demons, or faeries, or sprites. Yet even these agents, freed of their makers, act of their own accord. Even as vampires, without Sin, have endured and become what they've become."

"And you want to put us under the thumb of a god, to do his bidding?"

"Not at all. I simply want you to realize your true potential, to fulfill your true purpose. My husband no longer has his worshippers. He has had no designs or plans for centuries. As the mother of your kind, however, I simply wish the best for my children. You are my legacy. Unlike my husband, I was born and died a human. Call it nostalgia, if you will, but I still hold out hope that my children might fulfill their original purpose. My husband, distant though he may be, still loves me beyond death. He supports my end and has agreed to take an interest in the world again. After all, while the moon may be revered by many, according to many names and traditions, along with the sun it is the one force that reveals itself to all mankind. If the true path, the path that unites light and darkness, reflecting the character of my husband and the moon, is honored again so is he. Even if not by name."

I pinched my chin. "If the moon is such a marvelous force, and your husband is some kind of lunar deity, what does he have to do with werewolves? Surely, since they only change under a full moon, there's a connection."

"They are also my children. There is a reason vampires who do not master the path are susceptible to their bites. The wolves were born to punish those of my children who would lose sight of their true purpose, to keep my first-born children in check should their bloodlust consume them."

"How do I use this power as a master of the path? How do I realize the full potential of the darkness and light reunited? Will I be immune to the effects of the werewolf's bite when I leave?"

"Samuel chose to master the dark path alone. He is immune. You chose the nobler path, the one I hoped you would. You are not yet a master. Not yet. Should you prevail, and destroy the Van Helsing boy, you will be a true master. You will be one with the moon, therefore, one with the wolves."

"Good to know. Are you done with me here?"

"For now, child. For now. Go and do what you must. When all is done, when you've fulfilled your task, I will visit you again."

"You will visit me?"

"I am but a spirit, child. What you call a ghost."

"Will I be able to shift into a bat again? When I'm back on Earth?"

Ennigaldi nodded. "You've set foot on the path. Many abilities will be realized in time as you advance on your journey. Still, you are not yet a master. Such abilities might come and go until you reach your potential. Do not rely on them. Rely on what you know already. If new abilities arise and serve you well, then consider it a gift and a sign that you're on the right path."

I pressed my lips together. "About Samuel. We stopped him before with a wolf's bite. I'm guessing that won't work again."

"And with his immortality elixir, a stake to the heart will only put him in a slumber. It will not kill him."

"Chop his head off, then?"

"That will not free his spirit. His body must be burned. That's the only way his spirit will be released, that he might be taken by the reapers and consigned to perdition."

I cleared my throat. "The reapers can't harvest supernatural souls."

"Most of them cannot. There is one, however, who might deliver his soul to the place he belongs."

"You're talking about Zoey."

"You will require her aid when the time comes to burn Samuel's body. It is essential that his spirit be sent to where it belongs."

CHAPTER TEN

Something sucked me out of the vision and back to the cold cobblestone floor of the Scholomance. I still had to get back to my body. I had to explain all of this to Dracula. I wasn't sure if I could trust the old priestess who claimed she was married to Sin. I chuckled thinking about it. Maybe it was just a coincidence, but the notion of a god named Sin was ripe for jokes. I didn't dare tell any to the priestess, though. When it comes to jokes associated with someone's name, chances are they've heard them their entire lives and don't see the humor in them. I had a friend in high school named Heaven. Inevitably, every guy who ever took an interest in her tried to work her name into a cheesy pickup line. Sort of like my name, ever since Toyota came out with that damn van. How many guys can ride a Sienna at once? I bet she gets great gas mileage—in bed. All you've got to do is push the right button and her back door will pop right open. You get the idea.

So, no Sin jokes. Not around his ghostly human wife, at least. If I told Dracula about all this, there'd be no holding him back. He was the daddy of all dad jokes. He thought he was hilarious. Then again, I'm not sure I'd ever met a man who *didn't* think he was the next great comic just waiting to be discovered. You'd think after a few centuries of telling bad jokes Drac would get a clue, but being oblivious to his corniness was half of his charm.

I took a moment in the cold chambers of the Scholomance to consider my next move. My goal had been to find Abraham, clear the air, and move Dracula's priorities from ghost hunting to the hunters. Now the issue was a lot more complex. Hunters were still a problem. The Van Helsing brothers were still alive. Samuel Van Helsing was back. The ghost of Abraham Van Helsing had left the Scholomance with his son.

Ennigaldi made it clear that from her perspective, my priority should be to eliminate Samuel Van Helsing. Fair enough. How could I do that, though, without also dealing with his brothers, all the hunters who followed their lead, and his ghostly father? It was all a package deal, and not the good kind of bundle that let you get two streaming services for one low price. This package was short on bargains, long on shit. I was preparing to leave the Scholomance and go back to the schoolhouse with not much more direction about what to do next than I'd already had. I hadn't known that Samuel or Abraham was on Earth. I had hoped to prove Dracula's anxieties wrong. Now I knew he was right. How long ago had they left the Scholomance? Hard to say, since time there didn't match with the real world.

All I could do was look up the one figure among all of them who *might* leave a public footprint. Samuel Van Helsing, using the alias Dean Carver, was the Lieutenant Governor-elect. If he showed up anywhere, it would be national news. It was hard to believe that he wouldn't get back to his old plans, unless his new plans were of even grander scope now that he'd mastered the dark path of the Scholomance. I wasn't sure his plans could get much grander than taking over the world's governments, but his methods could get more ambitious and direct. And if he was back, perhaps he could use his influence on the president to cause all kinds of problems.

I focused on anything I thought might help me get back to my body. Everything from my hopeful relationship with Dylan to my friendship with Zoey to the taste of blood. It wasn't working.

All I could do was wait until Euryale brought me back. Given how time passed in the void, a day in the real world could leave me stuck for weeks. What was I going to do with all that time?

I paced the halls. I couldn't get through the walls on either side following either path. I shouted out to the god who spoke to me before. No response. I tried to tap into whatever powers I might have gained as a result of entering the path to master the Scholomance, but I didn't know what I was doing. Nothing I tried worked. I couldn't change into a bat. I couldn't shift into a dog, either. The Scholomance was within the void. As I understood it, even if someone entered the Scholomance through the gate in Romania, they entered the same Scholomance. I didn't know if that meant they passed into the void or if the Scholomance in the real world was connected to the Scholomance in the void in some mystical way.

All I did know was that there wasn't a clear exit. The whole place was closed and contained in a few stone chambers.

I sat at the table where Abraham had presumably been playing Monopoly with Samuel before everything changed. It struck me that they'd abandoned the game without a clear winner. Did that mean Samuel was taken into the path of darkness suddenly? Whatever the case, Abraham and his son had been passing the time. All I could guess was that in the time they'd spent together, Samuel must have passed the initiation into the Scholomance. Those trials were no joke. If he passed the initiation, some time had passed before he was allowed to progress to the next level.

Perhaps Samuel was getting his ass handed to him in Monopoly. The horseman was sitting in the Boardwalk space with a hotel on it. I knew from experience, beating Abraham at Monopoly was a challenge. I couldn't imagine getting so angry about a game that Samuel might storm off and get sucked into the path like I was. Then again, some people take games way too seriously. Anything was possible.

Finally, my vision started to fade. That could only mean one thing. The next thing I knew my arms and legs were stiff as my body turned from stone to flesh.

"Welcome back," Euryale smiled at me. Her snake hair was covered again.

Athena cocked her head. "Something's changed. You've changed."

I nodded. "I know why you can't get into the Scholomance. It's not Hades. Another god has reclaimed the Scholomance and hopes to restore it to its original purpose."

Athena tilted her head. "The Scholomance was first founded based on an ancient magic that had its roots in the gods of Babylon."

I nodded. "I spoke to a moon god called Sin. He wants to reunite the paths of light and darkness. He believes I'm the key."

Athena looked thoughtful. "That makes more sense than you might realize. What of the Van Helsings?"

"They're gone. Nowhere to be found. I need to get back home. If Samuel is out there, he has to be stopped."

Athena narrowed her eyes and stepped back, then disappeared in a flash of light.

I tilted my head. "That was sudden."

Morty nodded. "She does that. Is there anything else I can do to help?"

I shook my head. "Unless you can reap Abraham Van Helsing and send him back, for now, I need to get home."

CHAPTER ELEVEN

Morty's portal sent me back to my room at the schoolhouse. I grabbed my phone from my pocket to check the news, but there were no updates about Dean Carver. If Samuel was back on earth, he hadn't made an appearance. I wasn't sure if that was a good thing or a bad thing, but it meant that, for now, he wasn't immediately resuming his original plan.

I had a contact in the White House. Since Samuel sired the president—a fact that was still unknown to the general public—I needed to make sure that everything was still copacetic. I shot off a text to my contact. As far as he knew, the president hadn't received any communication from Samuel, so at least that wasn't an immediate worry. I encouraged my contact to isolate the president and to encourage him not to take any calls. If Samuel couldn't contact the president, he couldn't exert his influence over him.

We only had a few hours before the wolves had to go out again. I rushed back to Dracula's room. He was lacing his boots when I walked in.

"Sienna! Where did you go? We were all worried."

"We need to talk."

I told Dracula about everything that happened at the Scholomance. It was hard to tell what he was more concerned about—that I'd been taken into the path and, along with him, was supposed to reunite the two sides of the Babylonian moon god's magic, or the fact that both Samuel and Abraham were no longer there.

When I finished, Dracula stood and rubbed his brow. Then he turned and placed his hand on my forehead.

"What are you doing? I don't think I have a fever."

"I'm sensing the magic within you. You're right. There is something different."

"I don't know what I can do with it. When I was in that vision I became a bat and shifted back into my usual form again, but that's the only experience I've had with it."

Dracula nodded. "It took me some time to master my abilities as well. The only reason I took to my light-side gifts so quickly was because it wasn't that different than what I'd done for centuries. It was almost like doing it backward. Like writing with my opposite hand. I knew how to do it, it was just a matter of practice, sort of like muscle memory."

"I checked in with the president's people. They haven't heard anything from Samuel. There's nothing on the news, either."

Dracula shook his head. "He's changed. As insidious as taking over the world's governments and infecting all the world's leaders with vampirism sounds, if he's truly embraced the dark path, I fear what he's planning now is even more grim."

"Hard to imagine things getting much worse."

"On the bright side, I might have a lead on Abraham."

"Really?"

"I called Zoey when I couldn't find you. All she knew was that she'd sent Morty to come get you and take you to see Abraham. When I told her my concern that Abraham might not be in the

Scholomance—a worry that's proven itself valid—she reached out to your medium friend, Delphine. Her flight landed about an hour ago. She should be here momentarily."

I chuckled. "Did you ask her to come because of Abraham or because of the ghosts at that asylum?"

Dracula smiled. "Both. I still want to help those spirits. It began as an opportunity to familiarize ourselves with the paranormal. I figured we needed to learn more to deal with Abraham. The more I've read about their story, the things that were done to those patients, and the fact that the dead doctor's ghost might still be terrorizing those spirits, it's about them, too."

I took a deep breath. How could I argue with that? Vengeful spirits of mentally ill persons whose doctor experimented on them, and might still be doing so, had been suffering for years. Something had to be done. How could we help them, though, when hunters were coming after us and Dylan's pack? How could we get involved in the horror that was going on at the asylum when the Van Helsings might be coming for us at that very moment?

"I understand. We still have to deal with the situation with the wolves, though."

Dracula shook his head. "It's handled."

"What do you mean 'it's handled'?"

"They left several hours ago. They're heading north. They hope to be out of the state before nightfall. They should be out of the range of the hunters."

I sighed. "Unless the hunters follow them. They could be watching the schoolhouse. If they saw the wolves leave, who's to say they aren't following them?"

Dracula shook his head. "I took your van. I drove them to a chartered bus north of the city. I made sure we weren't being followed."

I huffed. "I hope you're right."

"Do you really think the wolves are still a priority? The Van Helsing brothers know we're helping them. If you killed those men, and the Van Helsings found the bodies, they'll know it was a vampire kill."

"We don't know how many hunters there are working with the Van Helsings," I reminded him. "It's not that hard to imagine they'd send a couple after the wolves while the rest come after us."

"We'll be prepared for that. Go astral if you have to. Your ability to do that is probably the biggest reason the Van Helsings haven't attacked yet."

I shook my head. "I'm pretty sure they know about the black lights that can negate the power in my brooch."

"Which is why they will likely try to lure you out. They'll either try to get you under their lights, or bait you to attack and blast you with a crossbow bolt the second you materialize."

"You're still a target as well."

Dracula laughed. "I've been a target of the Van Helsings for centuries. I can handle myself. I know their tricks. My priority is keeping you safe. Especially if what the priestess in the Scholomance told you is true. There might be larger threats to the world than we ever anticipated. You and I together might be the key to fighting those threats."

I nodded. "She said that if the demons are released from Hades, Athena won't be able to rein them back in. We might be the last line of defense between the world and hell remaking itself on Earth."

Dracula nodded. "We have to play this carefully. The Van Helsings, Samuel and Abraham's ghost included, are gunning for us. We aren't just the hunted. We're also hunting the hunters. We have to find a way to get to Samuel and end him."

"We have to find him first."

"Delphine will be here any minute. My hope is that, as a

medium, she'll be able to make contact with Abraham, or at least find him."

"If we can find Abraham, we can find Samuel. Presuming they're together."

CHAPTER TWELVE

Delphine arrived by Uber. I was a little anxious about her safety as she walked from the car to the schoolhouse. She dragged a suitcase behind her that was almost as tall as she was.

Delphine was in her middle-to-late forties, a pretty woman, Black with long dreadlocks that reached the small of her back. She was petite, and couldn't have been more than a buck-fifteen soaking wet. The first time I met her, "Miss Delphine" was operating a small business of her own in downtown Kansas City where she gave palm readings, flipped tarot cards, and consulted the spirits of the deceased. All for a price, of course. A woman has to make a living somehow. If I didn't know any better, the old me would have assumed she was a fraud, but it didn't take long working with her to recognize that she was one of the most psychically gifted people I'd ever met. That was especially true when it came to contacting spirits. If Abraham Van Helsing was nearby, she'd find him.

She made it inside without incident. The Van Helsings might have been ruthless hunters, but so far as I knew, they didn't kill humans. So far as Alexander and Reginald Van Helsing went, at least. Since Samuel was also a vampire, I couldn't say the same for him. Given what Ennigaldi said he'd done when presented with the test in the desert, he was a well-practiced killer. In a similar vein to Jack the Ripper, he was once known as Sam the Carver. Hence, the alias he assumed as Dean Carver, Lieutenant Governor-elect. He chose a first name paired with a last name that paid homage to his homicidal past. What a blood-sucking politician!

We had to disarm all of the booby traps to allow Delphine inside, and Dracula re-armed them as I led her to one of our many empty rooms that was still furnished. It had been furnished for one of the werewolves who'd since been slain by hunters.

Delphine dropped her suitcase and opened her arms for a hug. "It's a delight to see you again, my dear!"

I grinned. "Likewise. How was the flight?"

"Bumpy. I had a window seat, and the man sitting next to me didn't understand the concept of personal space."

I chuckled. "I've been there."

"Next time, I'm definitely going for the aisle. I hadn't flown in years. They didn't even serve a meal! Not like I'm complaining. As I can recall, the food was always horrendous. Still, it was better than a bag of pretzels and a Sprite. I could really use a bite to eat before we get started."

"I think the wolves might have a few things in the kitchen you could eat. I'd offer you something of my own, but I don't have anything other than blood."

Delphine grinned. "Unfortunately, blood doesn't fit well into my vegan lifestyle."

"I think Dylan has some protein shakes in the fridge. He thinks they'll give him muscles."

Delphine raised one eyebrow. "He realizes he has to work out along with the protein for that to work, right?"

I laughed. "I'm not sure he does."

"If it's whey, again, not vegan."

I sighed. "Right. Wolves aren't naturally vegan, either. I think he might have some plant-based shakes, too."

"I don't require much, love. Just a piece of fruit will do. Perhaps a small salad."

I raised my index finger. "Salad won't happen. No one who lives here likes vegetables. I think we have apples."

"That would be lovely. If you'd grab me one while I set up my things I'd be grateful."

Delphine threw her suitcase on the bed and popped it open. I was surprised such a small lady could lift it so effortlessly. Only one small corner of her suitcase was dedicated to clothing and toiletries. The rest included candles, bags of various substances I couldn't identify, and trinkets that likely carried mystical properties.

I let her get to unpacking and setting up for whatever séance she was planning and went to the kitchen. I helped myself to a bottle that Dracula had marked as "philistine wine."

I figured Delphine needed a little time to prepare, so I decided to enjoy it. Rather than gulp it down all at once, I took a breath between swallows.

Little known fact: vampires don't *have* to breathe, but most of us do. Even Dracula. It's residual human instinct. It also had the benefit of clearing my palate a bit between gulps. Dracula said there was an art to it if you wanted to bring out all the flavorful notes of a good blood-wine. I wasn't much of an artist. I didn't use fine brushes and didn't have the patience for detail that Rembrandt, Picasso, or Leonardo DaVinci must have had. I was more like my father when he painted my room when I was a girl. A big roller. Get as much paint on the wall as fast as possible with minimal spillage. The same principle applied to the difference between how Dracula and I enjoyed our blood. Same medium. Totally different approach.

Dracula could have nursed a bottle over the course of an evening. I downed one in less than five minutes. I burped. Didn't taste much different on the way up than on the way down. Double the pleasure. Double the fun.

When I got back to Delphine's room with her apple, she wasn't done setting up, but I was impressed with how much she'd done in such a short amount of time. Almost as impressed as I was that she'd fit so much crap in her suitcase.

At least twenty candles were scattered around. Back at her shop, or lair, or whatever it is you call a place where a medium does readings, she had big, thick, candles. These were long and thin. She'd also unfolded a plastic mat that was a lot like the giant Ouija-type summoning board she used the last time I'd required her services.

"How about that." I smirked. "Never would have thought that mediums have travel kits."

Delphine grinned. "I'm a medium who lives large. I like to take my show on the road."

Dracula stepped in right behind me. "Are we ready to begin?"

"Just about." Delphine moved a few candles an inch this way or that way and set trinkets around the room. She called them talismans, but I wasn't sure what the difference was. Talisman just sounded more expensive.

Everything had to be just so. There was probably an art, if not a science, to it. Whatever the case, I didn't bother asking questions. I might have some cool abilities, but I was about as sensitive as a brick. At least I was *before* what happened at the Scholomance. The only ghosts I ever saw were those who wanted me to see them. Sure, I'd seen more ghosts than the average person, and probably more than the ghost hunters on television. Most of that came with the territory of being friends with the Grim Reaper's sister. Before I'd met Zoey, I'd never seen anything more unusual than the kid in first grade who ate his boogers. Not that strange, I know. Everyone knew a kid who did that. But he was still doing it in high school.

Delphine started lighting her candles. You'd think she'd use one of those things that acolytes use with the extendable wick in churches, or something fancy. Instead, she pulled a butane lighter from her pocket. She was lighting the candles with the same thing she used to light her cigarettes.

Reverence might have its place in churches, but it wasn't necessary for a séance. She was contacting dead people, not gods. In my experience, most of the gods didn't deserve much reverence, either. A lot of them were dicks.

"Is there anything we can do to help?" I asked.

Delphine shook her head. "No offense, love. You're vampires. You're different. You might just scare the spirits away."

"Because we consume human blood?"

"No, doll. Mortal spirits don't resonate with your immortal privilege."

I huffed. "We aren't immortal. We *can* be staked."

"Please, child. Human life is fragile. There are thousands of ways a person can die. There's *one* way you can die. That some of you are foolish enough to get yourself staked doesn't make you mortal. It makes you stupid."

Dracula laughed. "Well, the whole blood-sucking thing tends to attract powerful enemies."

"There's plenty of blood out there," she pointed out. "You don't have to be an ass about how you go about getting it."

"Indeed," Dracula said. "That's why I strictly drink bottles and bags these days."

My eyes shifted back and forth. Delphine didn't know about my recent feeds. Sure, the hunters might have had it coming, but there was a certain degree of stupid involved in feeding from a person who was most likely to end my existence. Especially since those hunters had friends. Then again, sometimes stupidity is called for, especially when it's done in the name of saving one's friends.

I cleared my throat. "All right. So we sit back and watch. Got it."

Delphine turned to Dracula. "You wanted my help to communicate with the spirits trapped in that asylum, correct?"

Dracula nodded. "And to discern the whereabouts of Abraham Van Helsing's ghost."

"Certainly, dear. I haven't forgotten."

"Focus on Van Helsing first," I added.

Delphine smiled. "Of course."

She sat in the middle of her candles and placed a marble on her summoning board. Her eyes rolled back in her head.

"What's wrong?" I asked.

"Give me a moment."

Dracula and I waited. With each second, Delphine's face grew tenser and more strained. She shook her head. "I'm sorry. I can't find him."

"Does that mean his ghost isn't here?" I asked.

Delphine shook her head. "It means I can't find him. I consulted with several other spirits as well. None of them had any sense of his presence."

"Could that just mean he's not in New Orleans?" Dracula asked.

"The real essence of spirits is not bound to location. He's either not on Earth at all or he's using his power to conceal his presence."

Dracula nodded. "That's certainly possible."

Delphine clutched her head. "It's the other spirits. The ones at the asylum. I contacted them before. They're screaming at me."

Delphine raised both hands over her head. The marble moved on her summoning board.

D. I. E. D. I. E. D. I. E.

"They want to kill us?" I asked.

Delphine shook her head. "No. They want to die."

"Aren't they already dead?" Dracula asked.

"There's death, and then there's death. They want their suffering to end."

"What about the doctor?"

"He's there. His spirit is warped. Deranged. He's dominating the other spirits. He's threatening us."

"What is he saying?"

The marble moved again.

Y. O. U. A. R. E. M. I. N. E.

"What does that mean?"

Delphine shook her head. "He wants you to come back. He wants new patients. He's chosen you."

"He intends to kill us?" I asked.

"And if you don't come to him, he wants you to know he'll come for you."

I huffed. "Fuck."

CHAPTER THIRTEEN

I wasn't sure if I was more worried or pissed. If Dracula hadn't dragged us to that damn asylum, we wouldn't have the ghosts of the insane, and their even crazier doctor, gunning for us. I was still worried about the wolves. Samuel was out there somewhere. Abraham wasn't in the Scholomance, and it was unsettling that Delphine couldn't find him.

I thought having Delphine do her thing would give us direction and peace of mind. It was like going to a potluck and filling up your plate before you realize there are a half-dozen other dishes you need to try, so you pile it up and hope it doesn't fall off the plate and splatter all over the place. My plate was overflowing, but it wasn't with food. It was with shit. Don't ask me why anyone would put shit on a plate. The metaphor needs some work. The problem was that any of these enemies coming after us posed a legitimate threat. How could we possibly deal with them all at once, all while I was supposed to be hunting down Samuel per Ennigaldi's instructions?

To make matters worse, I couldn't understand how Dracula was so calm about it all. Maybe having been hunted as a monster for centuries and always evading the stake had something to do with it. This wasn't new for him. Then again, it wasn't like he'd ever been hunted by *immortal* Van Helsings, the ghost of another Van Helsing, and the dark-magic-wielding vampiric version of a Van Helsing. Not to mention a psychotic head-shrinking ghost who wanted to commit us to his asylum of the dead. On top of all that, Dracula had sent the werewolves off to the north for the night imagining they'd be fine. I wasn't sure if he was experienced and confident, or if his experience had made him over-confident and his cavalier attitude about it all would doom the both of us.

I paced around the room while Dracula and Delphine discussed ways to deal with vengeful spirits. Dracula had a little experience dealing with them and had a few methods, but Delphine knew more about dead folk than just about anyone I'd ever met. Even more than Mortimer Grimm, the Grim Reaper himself. She was more than a well of information, and she *knew* dead people, personally. She could speak to any ghost around the world who was willing to talk. She could use her vast network of spirits to find a ghost, like Abraham Van Helsing, if he was lurking anywhere in the earthly realm.

"There's no sure-fire way to put a spirit to rest against its will, " Delphine explained. "Every spirit that wanders the world is tethered here to something. It's a lifeline or, better, a death-line that holds them here. It's usually tied to whatever led the spirit to flee his or her reaper at the time of death."

I stopped pacing. "What if we could find the reaper who was originally assigned to this head-shrink?"

Delphine shrugged. "The reaper might know something but, then again, reapers are busy. Most of them have several assign-ments every day."

I shook my head. "Trust me. I know from Zoey. When a soul escapes, it leaves a black mark on a reaper's permanent record. That means there must be something we can find out about this doctor."

Delphine pinched her chin. "It's worth a try. However, you should be prepared, that even if we learn what it is that tethers the doctor to this world, severing his spirit from that tether might not be easy. It's one thing if a spirit is tied to an object or even their buried body. Burn it and the spirit's existence will release something like a homing beacon to the reapers. They'll come for him. It's more difficult if the tether is an idea or a cause. That is most often the case when it comes to vengeful spirits."

I tilted my head. "It sounds to me like experimenting on his patients is his cause. I'm not so sure if he's a vengeful spirit so much as a demented one."

Delphine shook her head. "He certainly gives off a vengeful vibe."

"That's because his patients killed him," Dracula put in. "Perhaps it's both vengeance and his commitment to his experiments that tethered him to this world. If that's the case, the key to dealing with the doctor might be to free his patients first. We have to find out what is tethering *them* and once they are gone, the doctor won't have a tether."

"That's not necessarily true," Delphine said. "His patients represent the object of his vengeance, but also his commitment to his experiments. That he threatened to kill the two of you and commit you to his asylum of the deranged dead suggests that releasing the patients might only be one step in the process."

I nodded. "Still, it's a necessary step."

Dracula looked hard at me. "Sienna, are you on board with this? I thought you were committed to focusing on the Van Helsings?"

"I am. The problem is that we don't know where Abraham or Samuel might be. They'll reveal themselves eventually. Until they do, I'd rather get this problem off our plate so we don't have to deal with it at the same time we're fighting the Van Helsings later.
"

Dracula scratched his head. "Delphine, can you tell us for certain if we're dealing with poltergeists?"

Delphine shrugged. "It's certainly possible. I cannot sense them the way I can human spirits. What I can say, though, is that so long as any poltergeists are contained within the confines of the old asylum, there's not much harm in leaving them there if the spirits manifesting them are released. Poltergeists will only migrate if their originating spirits bring them elsewhere. Otherwise, while the poltergeist might persist even after the spirit is gone, they'll remain where they're left. It might make the old asylum unusable for the foreseeable future unless the poltergeists are dealt with, but that's not your concern."

Dracula nodded. "You're right. The mental hospital there now isn't using the old building. I suspect it's because of the activity there that they haven't renovated or repurposed the facility."

I pulled out my phone. "If we're seriously going to do this, I'd like to get it done as soon as possible. The easiest way to contact Morty is through Zoey. He told me before he'd help however he could. I don't think he expected we'd be calling on him again so soon, but I'm sure he'll give us whatever information we need. Provided he has it, of course."

CHAPTER FOURTEEN

I made the call. I mentioned in passing that I might need Zoey to help to deal with Samuel Van Helsing. So long as we could incapacitate him, even if we had to haul his body back to Kansas City with his head in a separate box, she said she'd help if she could. Her due date was approaching and, even after the baby was born, it was a lot to ask a new mother to make a trip so soon. Still, it wouldn't take much effort if we brought Van Helsing to her to summon her scythe and reap his supernatural ass straight to hell. I'd even hold the baby for her when she did it—if the baby was born when the time came. Besides, I intended to make a trip back after the baby came anyway. I was going to be Auntie Sienna, after all. That was another bridge to cross. For now, I wanted to get this situation with the asylum and the crazy shrink off our plate as soon as possible, ideally before the night's end.

Zoey agreed to pass the message on to Morty. Less than fifteen minutes after I got off the phone with her, Morty showed up at the doorway to Delphine's room.

"You called?"

I laughed. "You must've portaled to my room."

Morty nodded. "I did. Zoey said you're looking for information on a wandering spirit."

Dracula had a file folder tucked under his arm. He handed a copy of an article to Morty. "Doctor Quentin Feuerhahn. Also, any of the other spirits who might be trapped at this location."

Morty nodded. "I can use the date of the article as a reference. I'm sure I have a file that details the incident."

"Cool. We'll be here."

Morty grinned and formed a portal out of thin air. He reached into it and pulled out a thick manilla folder. "So will I."

I was impressed. "Your files must be well organized."

Morty nodded. "All the old ones are. My father was a lot better at that sort of thing than I am. You wouldn't believe the stack of paperwork on my desk that needs sorting. Carmilla said she'd take care of it for me, but she's almost as busy as I am. When you're in the death and dying industry, you never get a holiday or day off. Damn humans keep dying every day."

I snorted. "Yeah. Damn those humans for dying all the time."

Morty cradled the folder in one arm and flipped through it with his opposite hand. "Quentin Feuerhahn, right?"

Dracula nodded. "That's right."

Morty sighed. "Well, it looks like my father handled that case himself. He was the Grim Reaper at the time, of course. It's pretty astounding that the spirit got away. I don't think my father lost more than a handful of spirits himself during his entire tenure. He was good. Better than I am."

"Then your father will remember him, right?"

Morty nodded. "I'm sure he will. Now that my dad has ascended, though, and is a god in Olympus, it might take me a little time to get to him. I can't say he'll be willing to come help, though. Bringing a god to Earth is complicated."

I nodded. "I remember. He'd need a golem to possess."

"It doesn't matter," Morty assured me. "I'll find out everything I can and be back in a couple hours."

Delphine raised her finger. "The most important thing is to learn what tethers the doctor to this world. Also, if your father knows more, what holds the spirits that are also trapped in the asylum."

Morty nodded. "I'll see what I can find out."

Morty left through a portal, and Delphine sat back down. She wanted to try to isolate some of the spirits in the asylum, to try to reach out to them apart from the doctor's oppressive influence, but she couldn't. Any time she reached out to one of the ghosts trapped in the asylum, the ghost of Doctor Feuerhahn got between them.

"Have you ever seen something like this before?" I asked.

Delphine took a deep breath. "There are often dominating spirits that oppress others around them. The hold this doctor has on those patients, though, is stronger than anything I've ever encountered."

Dracula rubbed his brow. "If the doctor is a vengeful spirit, you'd think his focus would be on the patients who killed him. I'm guessing a lot of those spirits are those he killed through his experiments."

Delphine nodded. "I can't say for certain, because I can't isolate those spirits to hear what they have to say. It's possible that vengeance is what tethers them all together. The ghosts murdered by the doctor want vengeance but can't overcome him. Some of the spirits may be those who killed the doctor. We just don't know. Still, it's also possible that the doctor is directing his vengeance at any patient he'd ever treated, blaming them all rather than individuals for what happened. Vengeance is rarely rational."

I stayed with Delphine while Dracula left to reinforce some of the booby traps. His old castle in Transylvania was littered with traps, which was one reason he managed to survive for so long even though Van Helsing and the hunters who came after him knew exactly where he was. He was limited now, as some of the booby traps he'd used in Transylvania were invigorated by the dark power he used to wield. So far, he hadn't figured out a good way to replicate similar traps using the light-side power. I might have been able to help with that, now that I'd dipped my toes into the dark-side powers, but I wasn't a master yet.

I pulled up an old classroom desk and dinked around on my phone while Delphine continued trying to get in touch with the spirits from the asylum. From the look on her face, she wasn't enjoying herself. I decided to catch up on my social media since I had neglected my accounts for a while. I had a half-dozen friend requests, mostly old high school friends looking to re-connect.

I had a message from my father. My parents and I weren't exactly close. My dad ran off with a younger woman when I was twelve, and my mother spent the rest of my teenage years bouncing from man to man—sometimes literally. They were under the impression I'd moved to New Orleans on a scholarship to pursue my computer science degree. They didn't know a thing about what I was really up to. They didn't even know I'd become a vampire. I came up with excuses not to come home for holidays. Not like either of them had big plans, anyway.

My dad's message was simple and to the point. He'd sent it almost a week before and I hadn't noticed.

I miss you. How are you doing?

I sent back an equally brief response.

MIss you too. I'm good. How are you?

Other than that, my newsfeed was full of cat pictures, people virtue signaling about their healthy lifestyles by posting pictures of their kale and quinoa meals, and an endless collection of memes.

It struck me as odd how I used to practically live on social media. Now, I hardly ever checked it, and I didn't miss it. I might have developed a habit of sucking blood, but those apps were soul-sucking.

I glanced back at Delphine. She looked awfully uncomfortable, with an expression someone might have if they'd been on the toilet for twenty minutes and still couldn't go. A combination of exhaustion and determination. Not that I'd seen a lot of people in that situation. I'm not a weirdo. But who hasn't been there?

It was a relief when Morty's portal appeared again in the room. Had two hours already passed? Maybe. Didn't seem that long. Whatever the case, he'd made good time.

Morty was always dressed fancy since he'd become the Grim Reaper. Before that, when he was just Zoey's little brother, he'd sported a punk rocker vibe, mohawk and all. Now, he looked like the CEO of a Fortune 500 company. I suppose managing an entire world of reapers was a lot like being the CEO of a large corporation.

I pocketed my phone and got up from the desk. "What did you find out?"

"Where's Dracula? He'll want to hear this."

"Hey, Drac!" I cupped my hands around my mouth. "Morty's back!"

Dracula was back in the room about two seconds later. Vampires can move fast. "What did you learn?"

"The whole story is a bit crazy. I guess it makes sense. Asylum and all. So, my dad took the case himself, because several other spirits in the place had already run from their reapers. When the doctor himself turned up on the schedule, and the cause of death was murder, Dad knew it would be tricky."

I nodded. "I'm guessing it was even trickier than he anticipated."

"Definitely. So, my dad arrives on scene. Does his standard

recon. He said there were ten wandering souls tethered to the place already."

"Ten? And he couldn't just reap them then and there?"

Morty shook his head. "They weren't on the schedule. They were past due. Reap a spirit after his time, so long as he's still tethered, and the boatman can't take the soul. No admittance to heaven or hell. The only way for a wandering spirit to get back on the schedule is to break the tether. That's not something a reaper can do. It's beyond the job description."

"Could he tell what the tether was?"

Morty nodded. "It was the doctor. As you already surmised, these were vengeful spirits."

"You can say that again," Delphine put in. "Some of the worst I've ever tried to contact. They've been stuck for so long that I'm not sure they even know what vengeance they're seeking. They're full of rage, but it's not focused."

"That makes sense," Morty explained. "The longer a vengeful spirit lingers on Earth, the more they forget about their lives before. When their memories go, all that's left is a big bundle of pissed-off. They know they need vengeance but forget their target. So they take their anger out on anyone and everyone who gets close to them. Not because they like hurting people, but because they're desperate."

Delphine nodded. "Desperate to exact their vengeance. Every person they hurt or, heaven forbid, kill, represents a possible tether. That's why they begged us to kill them when I contacted them before. All they want is for their nightmare to end."

"Precisely. Anyway. The doctor *knew* about the spirits. Makes sense. If those ghosts were looking for vengeance, at least before they lost their memories, he was their target."

"How did your dad figure out that the doctor knew about the ghosts?" I asked.

"It was the salt and the ward he was wearing. Salt lines were poured around the perimeter of the doctor's office."

"What kind of ward?"

"A pendant of some kind. My dad didn't get a good look at it. The doctor kept touching it through his shirt. It radiated an energy that my dad could sense. Strange, because even the Grim Reaper doesn't feel just any kind of magic. It must've had some connection to the gods. It radiated an energy that repelled the spirits."

I cocked my head. "Why bother with salt if the doctor had a magical trinket that would do the job?"

Morty shrugged. "Magical items like that can only be used so many times before they have to recharge. It allowed him to move throughout the facility but he had to retreat to his office where the salt kept the spirits out so the trinket could get back to full strength. That's what my dad figured, anyway."

"It makes sense," Dracula mused. "Did your father get a good look at the trinket after the doctor died?"

Morty shook his head. "The patients who killed him stole it. When the doctor's spirit fled, my dad pursued him. Obviously, he got away, which was pretty impressive considering my dad's skill and power. Anyway, before my dad could get back to examine the body, the trinket was gone."

"The patients who killed him knew what it was?" I asked.

"Maybe," Morty said. "Or they thought it looked valuable and stole it to pawn. Whatever happened, the killers also took the doctor's keys and escaped."

I thought for a moment. "Perhaps the patients knew about the trinket and needed to escape. They knew the doctor's ghost would be after them."

Delphine pursed her lips. "With so many ghosts in the place, it's possible the patients who killed the doctor were acting under their influence. Spirit possession is possible. Considering that we're talking about a mental hospital, there were likely patients who didn't have the strength of mind to resist such a possession."

"If that was the case, killing the doctor didn't sever the tether.

Those ghosts are still trapped in the asylum," Dracula pointed out.

Delphine looked back to her summoning board. "Your father said there were ten spirits wandering the place at the time, correct?"

"That's right."

"I only sensed seven, at most."

I narrowed my eyes. "If the spirits were freed, they'd have been back on the schedule, right?"

Morty nodded. "My father would have known it. He would have told me about it."

Delphine sighed. "Those spirits might still be possessing those patients today."

I gulped. "How is that possible? Can a ghost possess someone that long?"

"They'd be pretty old now, but if those patients were out of their minds, it's not impossible."

Dracula still had the manilla folder in his hand. "I have several patient files here. If we can cross-reference the files with the patients we know are dead, and figure out if any of them went missing but are still alive, we might be able to track them down."

"Why would we do that?" I asked. "How would that help us?"

"The doctor is tethered to them. He won't leave until he has vengeance or his tether is broken somehow. The other spirits he's oppressing were murdered by the doctor. They're bound to him. If we can break the doctor's tether, we might be able to free all of them."

I frowned. "That might mean bringing three very old people back to the asylum and letting the doctor kill them. How can you even suggest that?"

"Technically they're already dead," Delphine clarified. "At least, the spirits possessing those bodies are dead. The poor afflicted souls who those bodies belong to have been imprisoned by those spirits for years."

"You really think their bodies are still alive?" I asked.

"A spirit who possesses someone fills the body with their energy. In theory, these patients might not appear old at all. They might not look much older than they did when all this happened."

"Sort of like how Roy was a ghost but now inhabits a golem."

"Right," Morty agreed. "He's basically immortal now. A human body can function *like* a golem. The moment we exorcise those ghosts from their bodies, though, there's no telling what will happen to the original spirits in the bodies. They won't be of sound mind. Their bodies might age rapidly, or maybe their bodies will start to age normally. This is sort of uncharted territory."

"It is," Delphine added. "In all my years, I've never encountered a spirit that possessed a body for more than a few days. They usually leave once they've accomplished their goal."

"But they did accomplish their goal," I reminded her. "They *killed* the doctor."

Dracula shook his head. "Maybe that wasn't their goal. They left because they wanted to trap the doctor there just as they were before. They knew if he couldn't get his vengeance, he'd be stuck as a ghost in that asylum forever."

I tucked a strand of my hair behind my ear. "If their idea of vengeance is to torment the doctor's ghost indefinitely, how can that tether ever be broken?"

"I can't say for sure," Delphine replied. "But perhaps once the doctor's spirit is gone, and their vengeance is no longer possible, it will also break the tether. It won't satisfy their vengeance, but their vengeance as they envisioned it would no longer be possible.

"Right," Dracula said. "Therefore, no more tether. If that works, it might suffice to free every spirit in that place."

"I can help with the research," Morty offered. "I need a list of patients. No need to go searching for obituaries. I can check the schedules back in the underworld. If there are names in those files whose spirits have *never* come due for harvest, we'll know they're still out there."

I nodded. "And we'll know who those lost spirits are possessing."

CHAPTER FIFTEEN

I expected Morty to browse Dracula's stolen medical files, hightail it back to the underworld, and report his findings. Instead, he examined the files then reached through a portal and pulled a few files of his own back through.

He wasn't joking when he said his father's old files were well organized. What is it about older folks and their ability to keep paperwork in order? Maybe it's because the younger generation relies on digital storage. As I understood it, Morty was in the process of trying to do the same. Sure, there wasn't an internet in the underworld, but there's still a lot someone can do with a computer without Wi-Fi. These were old-school records, filed and cataloged, rarely consulted. Why would anyone have reason to examine records nearly a century old?

Morty and Dracula pulled over a couple of desks to cross-reference their notes and finally came up with the names of three former patients whose files were closed without remark. Men who, according to Morty, had never been reaped.

Mitchell Bergland. Garret Schumer. Daniel Rhodes.

Morty grinned. "Collectively, by first name: MGD."

I raised an eyebrow. "Miller Genuine Draft?"

"It's a classic. You know me. I love my brewskis."

I grabbed my phone to search for MGD. Not the beer. The three shoulda-been-dead dudes. The spirits possessing those men weren't Mitchell, Garret, or Daniel, but it was reasonable to guess that they'd assume the identities of the bodies they possessed. Even cross-referencing patients who died in the asylum with Morty's reaper records didn't tell us for sure which ghosts possessed MGD. A lot of loose spirits who'd evaded their reapers were running around in that asylum. Their memories were so warped that Delphine couldn't tell us their names, either. Ultimately, it didn't matter. The spirits possessing MGD were the ones who killed the doctor. They were the targets of his vengeance. To unravel the whole thing, we had to break Doctor Feuerhahn's tether and reap his demented ghastly ass to hell.

There wasn't any guarantee that the ghosts possessing MGD were still using their old names, though. If they didn't age, as Delphine predicted, it would be awfully strange for men who should have been older than a hundred to continue living under the same aliases. Then again, these were warped spirits, possessing the bodies of the mentally ill. There was no telling what they'd been up to all this time, or how clearly they were thinking.

My Internet search yielded three names that corresponded with MGD. They also happened to live in the same neighborhood: the historic Garden District.

The Garden District was home to the wealthiest families in New Orleans. It was the Beverly Hills of the city. The three men weren't only residing in the same neighborhood—but all within the same city block.

"This has to be them." I showed Dracula a map where I'd marked the locations of each of the men. "It can't be a coincidence that three men with these names happen to live in the same neighborhood."

Dracula nodded. "I agree. We should pay them a visit."

Morty tilted his head. "What exactly are you going to tell them? They need to give up their lives so the ghost of a doctor they once murdered can go to hell?"

Dracula shrugged. "Maybe they don't realize how the doctor is still terrorizing the patients there."

Delphine shook her head. "They might have some level of empathy for those spirits. I wouldn't count on it, though. It's one thing to have empathy, it's another thing to be willing to give up one's life for someone."

I nodded. "I'd be willing to bet that no one apart from these men knows the truth. Besides, these are spirits who were terrorized and tortured by the doctor. Can anyone blame them for what they did?"

"Not at all," Dracula said. "At the same time, they stole other people's bodies to do it. They might be victims, but so are the souls of the men whose bodies they took. We can't ask them nicely to come along. We're going to have to take them."

I sighed. "We're talking about abducting men who live in a wealthy neighborhood. We don't know anything about the lives they've built over the decades. From what I'm finding here, these men don't live alone. That means they have families."

Dracula nodded. "Families who likely don't know the truth."

"Does that matter?" I asked. "If these men have kids living at home, families who depend on them, we can't just take their fathers away."

Delphine sighed. "We can't leave the souls imprisoned in their bodies to languish forever."

"What if we table the whole thing?" I proposed. "We don't know for sure if the doctor can leave the asylum. He may not come for us at all."

Delphine bit her lip. "He knows where we are now. We made contact. He encountered you when you went to the asylum. Vengeful spirits can migrate."

"There's also a chance that one of the three men still has the doctor's trinket," Morty suggested. "That could come in handy. Not just for dealing with these spirits, but to handle Abraham Van Helsing if or when he comes after you."

Delphine pursed her lips. "That might give us an opportunity. It depends on how that trinket works. It may temporarily loosen the tethers that bind the vengeful spirits. I'm not sure if the trinket repels the spirits. It might also temporarily dispel the spirits."

I raised an eyebrow. "You can dispel a spirit?"

"That might not be the best word. Consider it more like putting the spirit in a temporary slumber. If that works, and we can put the doctor to sleep, we may be able to free the other spirits in the asylum."

Morty nodded. "We may get the green light to reap them before the doctor returns."

I shook my head. "That still wouldn't get rid of the doctor. He'd come back eventually. He'd still want vengeance on the ghosts possessing MGD."

Dracula shook his head. "Then we don't free the doctor. We don't send him to hell. We trap him instead."

"How do we trap a ghost?" I asked.

"The trinket might help with that," Delphine reasoned. "No matter how it works, a ghost can't get past it. We lure the doctor into a body. Allow him to possess someone, then strap the trinket on him. His spirit won't be able to leave. Then, we bury the body alive. Sink him to the bottom of the ocean. Whatever. It would be an eternity he'd deserve."

She hadn't accounted for one important detail. "Whose body is he going to possess?"

"We could make a golem," Morty said. "Don't you still have the crystal you and Zoey used back in Kansas City?"

I shook my head. "I left it with her."

"Not a worry," Morty assured me. "I can get another one."

"Even so, how do we know the trinket will hold him? If the thing has to recharge, he might be able to overpower it."

"Maybe," Delphine said. "He had to recharge the trinket because he had a host of spirits coming after him in the asylum. He's only one spirit. He might not be able to drain its power faster than it recharges."

I sighed. "That's the question of the day, isn't it? We can't know for sure. If we bury the doctor in a golem somewhere, who do you think he'll come after next?"

"He's already said he's coming for us," Dracula replied. "This might work in a way that doesn't require sacrificing the spirits who are possessing the men in the Garden District."

"It still doesn't do anything for the souls imprisoned in their bodies."

"Then we make more golems," Morty said. "We create new bodies that look just like the ones MGD are using. We convince the spirits possessing them to take their new golems and live out their lives."

Dracula nodded. "Then the souls will be free to reclaim their bodies and live out their lives."

CHAPTER SIXTEEN

The sun was setting on the horizon as we piled into my van and headed to the Garden District.

My mind drifted to Dylan and the wolves. I'd texted him a few times and he'd said they were fine, but I was still anxious. It's not like he'd know if any hunters were on his tail until he had one—and then, probably only after they took a shot.

Our plan to deal with the doctor and the asylum ghosts was complex. It had a lot of mights and maybes about it. Things were surmised that *could* be true, but weren't sure. For instance, even if we trapped the doctor in the golem, we didn't know if the trinket would hold him or for how long. We didn't know anything about the trinket other than that it was old and emitted an energy that repelled spirits. Morty thought that since his father detected the trinket's energy when he went to reap Doctor Feuerhahn, he might sense it if we were close. Not every reaper was sensitive to mystical energies, but *the* Grim Reaper had powers the others didn't. I knew Morty was able to cast trans-dimensional portals between the underworld and Earth anywhere he liked. Other reapers were dependent on the communal portals that were designed to take the reapers to their scheduled assignment sites.

It made sense that he might also be sensitive to other magics. He had to keep track of thousands of reapers as they navigated the world harvesting souls. Reapers weren't entirely human, but they weren't gods, either. You might think of the Grim Reaper as a demigod, and his reapers, demi-demigods. Not sure if that's a thing, but you get the point. One rung on the ladder lower than a demigod, but not human, either.

It was worth a shot. If Morty sensed it, his cloak allowed him to go astral with me. We could sneak into one of the MGD houses and snatch it. Of course, it would be better if they played along.

How sane these folk might be was another question. They were the spirits of former asylum patients. They'd also had nearly a century to get their shit together. Given that they lived in the Garden District, they'd not only gotten their shit together, but they were shitting gold.

Morty insisted on checking out each of the three residences before we tried to speak to them. A little recon never hurt. If he knew where the trinket was, we'd have to decide whether it was best to sneak in and take it or confront the possessing spirits and ask for it nicely. Would they comply? If they knew it would help us give Feuerhahn the eternal torment he deserved, maybe.

The Garden District had a lot of older mansions, many faced with white marble Corinthian columns. The grounds were perfectly kept. Enough to make any suburban father envious. These folk, I suspected, didn't do it by sweat and dedication. They probably hired landscapers.

We stopped in front of the first house. The "M" house. I didn't want to use their names. These men weren't the people to whom those names belonged. Morty stepped up to the house. He placed his hand on the front door and walked back to the sidewalk where Dracula, Delphine, and I waited.

"I don't sense anything here. Let's check the next one."

I heard a loud crash. Then breaking glass. It was coming from a couple of houses down. "I think that's the 'G' house."

We took off running as more bangs sounded from the house.

"I feel something," Morty reported. "An energy. This must be it."

Delphine tilted her head. "There's a spirit here."

"Is it the doctor?" I asked.

"If it is, he isn't acknowledging me. My abilities are limited without the right preparations. I can't say for sure, but it must be."

A kitchen chair went flying through the front window and landed not far from us along with broken glass.

"That resembles poltergeist activity," Dracula remarked. "Poltergeists are typically manifested by young females."

"So, this isn't the doctor? It's another of the patients?"

"No way to be sure," Delphine admitted. "But I'd say the doctor had a few mental quirks of his own."

"He might be possessing someone," Dracula said. "We have to get to him."

Delphine grabbed Dracula's arm. "Remember, I sensed a spirit. What if we're wrong about the trinket? What if it doesn't repel spirits but gives someone the ability to manipulate them? To control them."

"That would make sense," I mused. "What if that's what the doctor was doing all along with his experiments? What if the doctor tortured those patients because he was *trying* to turn them into vengeful spirits? What if he was using the trinket to keep them in check, to both protect himself from the spirits and to use them? Whatever it is, we need to get it. Ready to go astral, Morty?"

"I'll come in behind you," Dracula said. "Perhaps I can cause a distraction. A focal point for the poltergeists. Maybe for the doctor. If he's there, and he's serious about coming after us, I might be able to lure him away while you two get the trinket."

Morty made a quick portal and reached into it and grabbed his reaper cloak. He slipped it on over his suit, then raised his hood as I touched my brooch.

I followed Morty in the astral plane through the front door of the house.

Furniture was moving across the living room. I looked toward the kitchen and saw a dinner plate fly across the room like a frisbee and shatter against the wall.

"This way," Morty instructed. "The energy is coming from upstairs."

Dracula thought we were dealing with poltergeists. There must've been a lot of them, and they were only getting more aggressive. Every second we were in there, the banging, crashing, and smashing of virtually anything that wasn't mounted to a wall increased.

One of the banging sounds was probably Dracula busting through the front door. Or maybe he just climbed through one of the already broken windows.

Morty was following the energy like a bloodhound on a scent. We entered a large room.

A man stood in the center of the room. He wasn't entirely solid. His hair was gray, but he wasn't facing us. He turned his head to the side.

I gasped when I saw his profile. Could it really be?

I rubbed my eyes. When I did, the man was gone and the banging stopped.

Morty stomped his foot. "The energy. It's gone."

"Did you see that man?" I asked. "I didn't get a good look. For a second, though, I could have sworn it was Abraham Van Helsing."

CHAPTER SEVENTEEN

"You must've been mistaken," Dracula insisted. "This situation isn't connected to the Van Helsings."

I shook my head. "Unless Doctor Feuerhahn and Doc Van Helsing share a similar likeness, I wasn't mistaken."

"He wasn't a fully formed apparition," Morty pointed out. "Translucent and a little blurry. I can see why it might be easy to mistake his identity."

I rubbed my brow. "Maybe you're right. Still, it looked like Abraham. Just like I remembered him from my time in the Scholomance."

Morty stroked his chin. "More curious is how I sensed the energy while the activity was going on. When the energy dissipated, the poltergeists stopped and the apparition stopped. Something was emanating an energy like the one my father described. It may or may not be the same trinket that Feuerhahn was wearing before he died."

"It doesn't matter," Delphine placed her hand on my back. "It appears that of the two options we considered, the trinket doesn't silence spirits or put them in a slumber. If the trinket allowed someone to control the spirits, whoever was using the trinket could order them to leave at the same time he escaped the house with it."

I sighed. "I still have this sinking feeling that the ghost of Abraham Van Helsing was involved. I don't know why, or how."

"I'm not disputing that you think you saw what you saw," Dracula assured me. "Still, I cannot fathom why Abraham would be interested in this particular case. The spirits at the asylum and the doctor aren't linked to anything related to the Van Helsings. I originally brought up the case for no other reason than to give us some experience dealing with specters before we might have to confront Van Helsing's ghost."

"You're probably right," I acknowledged. "Maybe I was just seeing what I wanted to see. Do we have any pictures of Doctor Feuerhahn?"

Dracula nodded. "In my files. I left them back at the schoolhouse. If you only saw him from behind, however, a suit from a bygone era would fit Feuerhahn as well as Abraham Van Helsing. Either way, we didn't get the trinket. I have no idea where the person is who is supposed to live in this place. We still have two other houses. Perhaps if 'G' is off the table, 'M' or 'D' might be able to give us information if we present to them our solution. Give them new bodies if they can help us cast the doctor into a golem."

I nodded. "I've programmed a few of those archeus crystals. We can sweeten the pot and add a few enhancements to the golems if necessary."

We checked the other two houses. They were also vacant. We didn't see any signs of a struggle at either of the other two houses. They were just empty. Were MGD gone before the spirits and poltergeists appeared? Where were they? The houses and rooms were furnished in a way that suggested that these men had families, including children. *Everyone* was gone. Morty double-checked the reaper schedules to make sure that no last-minute additions had been made. He found nothing, which meant they were still alive somewhere. But where? Why were they gone? Did they know we were coming? I'd hoped by the end of the night we'd be able to put this whole situation with the vengeful spirits behind us. Instead, everything was more complicated. Whoever took that trinket, presuming that's what was responsible for the energy Morty sensed, now had the ability to command spirits.

CHAPTER EIGHTEEN

I didn't bother texting Dylan. At this time of the night, they were already wolfed out, and paws don't do well on touch screens. I wouldn't know for sure if he and the other wolves made it through the night until morning.

We all climbed into my van, and we headed back to the schoolhouse.

Dracula always went in first so he could disarm the booby traps. When he opened the door he turned and closed it again.

"The traps have all been triggered."

I tilted my head. "I presume that means we have bodies, or at least some blood in the hall?"

"That's the thing. There's nothing."

"Spirits," Delphine guessed. "Perhaps an intelligent ghost, maybe a poltergeist. It wouldn't be hard to trigger the traps."

"We had the whole place covered in salt! If any spirits got in, they must've come in through the ground or the roof."

"Or a ghost possessing a body wouldn't be thwarted by salt. That would explain how the traps were triggered."

"My traps are solid," Dracula insisted. "A ghost in a body

would still be vulnerable to my traps. I don't think they'd get through unharmed."

I looked at Morty. "Should we go astral and scout out the place again?"

"There are spirits inside," Delphine cautioned. "I can't say who or how many."

"Do you think it could have been the same spirits we just encountered at the house? If the doctor claimed a body and is commanding spirits, he could have sent them in to trigger the traps before entering himself."

Delphine considered this. "It's certainly possible. While we were investigating the other houses in the Garden District, there was enough time that they could have come here and disarmed the traps."

"No need to scout out the place," Dracula proposed. "We know there are spirits inside. We have iron weapons in the van. We should arm ourselves and go in prepared."

I opened the back of the van. Dracula had a couple of iron swords he'd purchased from antiquity dealers, and a few iron fire-pokers. When it came to dealing with ghosts, it was the iron, not the shape or sharpness of the weapon, that mattered. Iron wouldn't kill or free a spirit, but it would force one that had materialized to dissipate. As I understood it, they'd have to gather usable energy to manifest again. Whatever energy they could draw from they'd use. They drew on heat, which was what caused cold spots in rooms where spirits manifested. They could drain your phone battery or draw from the electricity flowing to the lights, which was why they often flickered when ghosts were active.

We made our way through the schoolhouse. Drac and I carried the swords. Delphine and Morty each wielded an iron poker. Delphine sensed a host of presences throughout the facility, but they weren't engaging us. Perhaps they knew to steer clear seeing that we had iron weapons in hand.

I scanned the perimeter of the building, checking all the windows and doors. Some of the salt-infused paint had been scratched off one of the windowsills.

"Dracula, take a look at this."

Dracula peered at the spot. "Curious. It certainly would make it easier for the spirits to get inside. The question is how did someone get in the place to scratch off the paint to begin with?"

"Allow me to return to my circle," Delphine suggested. "Perhaps now that we know the spirits are here and I have the aid of my devices, I can reach out to them and learn more."

We followed Delphine back to her room, but Morty stopped halfway there in the middle of the hallway. He raised his hand just over his shoulder.

"What is it?" I asked.

"That energy. I sense it. I can't say if it's the trinket, but it's the same energy I felt at the house before."

I bit one side of my bottom lip. "The trinket can't be wielded *by* a ghost, right? So if the doctor has it, he's still possessing a body and he's here."

"Whoever is controlling it is here," Delphine agreed. "We cannot rule out the possibility that it might be someone else."

"Like MGD?" I asked.

"They are possessed bodies. They have reason to manipulate the spirits, especially that of the doctor, but I do not know why they'd consider coming here."

Dracula nodded. "Which is why we must assume it is the doctor possessing someone else."

Delphine went into her room. Her summoning circle was still set up and she re-lit her candles. "I'm going to try and find out what I can."

Dracula looked up and down the hall. "We should search the premises. If the trinket is here, there's someone holding it. If we can take it by force we can end this once and for all."

"Give me a moment first," Delphine urged. "You should know what you're looking for."

Dracula grunted. He was eager to get on with the search. Delphine had a point, though. It was best to have a little intel on what the spirits in the schoolhouse were up to before we went charging through the halls looking for whoever was wielding the trinket. After all, if that trinket allowed someone to command the spirits, it was best we took whoever had it by surprise. Going astral would help. Dracula roaring through the halls and spreading his cloak while flashing his fangs probably wouldn't. It might frighten maidens who feared the count's bite, but whoever we were facing wasn't going to be intimidated by Drac's vampiric-stalker routine.

Delphine sat cross-legged in the middle of her circle. "There's still a spirit who is shielding himself from me. There's a power about him I cannot penetrate."

I raised an eyebrow. "The doctor?"

"Perhaps. But if it is the doctor, who is wielding the trinket?"

Dracula tugged at his ear. "How could that doctor shield himself from us? Just because he had a magic item doesn't mean he knew magic that could empower his spirit beyond the grave."

"I can't say," Delphine admitted. "All I know is what I feel. I cannot give you answers when the spirits refuse to speak."

"Can you ask any of the other spirits what we're dealing with?"

Delphine shook her head. "Whoever is in control of that trinket will not permit them to speak."

Dracula and I moved through the halls with our swords in hand. Delphine and Morty followed close behind with their iron pokers.

The spirits were making a lot of noise, just like at the house before. Maybe it wasn't poltergeists, or perhaps the spirits there were able to bring their poltergeists with them. Whatever the case, the school was a good-sized building. Several hallways intersected. Every time we got closer to the sounds, the bangs moved further ahead of where we were. It was like they were toying with us, leading us around the place just because they could.

We tried to split up, but since ghosts aren't bound to the material world the way we were, it wasn't doing much good. If we cornered them, they could stay invisible to us and float right past. It takes a lot of energy for a ghost to appear. They don't show up unless they want to.

Eventually, everything quieted down.

"Are they gone?" I asked.

Delphine shook her head. "They're still here. They just aren't making any noise."

"Any better idea how many we're dealing with?"

"The more they know I'm working with you, the less likely they are to respond when I reach out. I can't force spirits to manifest or communicate. It's always by choice. All I can say is that we're dealing with a fair number of ghosts. There may be some poltergeists, too, but I can't say for sure. But it's enough that it might include all seven remaining former-patient spirits at the asylum."

Dracula huffed. "I'm going to go reset the traps. We'll deal with the ghosts when they decide to come out to play. If we can't get to them or the trinket, there's not much we can do to help them move on. Do you still sense the energy from the trinket, Morty?"

Morty felt around for a moment. "It's subtle all the time so I didn't even notice it. I think it's gone."

"It should be fine," Delphine put in. "The doctor might have these spirits in his thrall, but if he has the trinket and he's possessing a body that's no longer here, the spirits are relatively free. They have no vendettas against us."

"*Relatively* free?" I asked.

"They aren't free to move on, if that's what you mean. They are free from the doctor's oppressive influence."

Dracula was already walking away from us. He waved his hand at us over his shoulder. "Like I said, I'm re-setting the traps. If the doctor is in a body and he tries to get back in, we'll catch him."

CHAPTER NINETEEN

Dracula was having a hell of a time getting the traps to reset. Every time he had them ready they'd go off again. It was probably the ghosts lingering in the schoolhouse. Delphine said it didn't mean that the spirits were acting vengefully. They might have just been screwing around. She still couldn't get them to talk.

It was for the best, as Dylan and the other wolves had just pulled up outside. They'd made it back safe.

I took a deep breath, as if an anvil had just been lifted off my chest. Then another car pulled up behind them. A black Mustang. The doors opened and Alexander and Reginald Van Helsing stepped out.

"What the hell?" I asked as Dylan approached, his hand raised as if his palms had the magical ability to stop me from ripping those hunters' heads off.

"Hear them out, Sienna."

I narrowed my eyes. "There's no way I'm trusting you two."

Alexander pressed his lips into a close-mouthed grin. "I'm a Van Helsing, coming to Dracula and the infamous daywalker for help. You aren't the only one with trust issues."

I smirked. "Did you just say 'the *infamous* Daywalker? Hey, Drac! Did you hear that? I'm *infamous* now!"

"Congratulations?"

"All right, Alex. What brings you here?"

Alexander cleared his throat. "Alexander, please."

I shrugged. "Sorry, man. Just trying to keep things casual. You know, in the spirit of friendship."

Alexander huffed. "You killed our brother. You killed two more hunters as of late. Friendship has nothing to do with this. Only necessity."

"We're on a mission from our father," Reginald piped up.

"Our brother is out of control," Alexander added. "He had a plan to enslave our father's ghost. Our father appeared to us last night to warn us in advance. He also said that you, Sienna, might be the only one who can stop him and free our father."

I scratched my head. "Stopping Samuel is on my agenda, don't get me wrong. How do I know that you two won't stake me the second it's done?"

"My father begged us to consider a truce," Reginald explained. "Too much blood has been shed in the name of an ancient vendetta. You are not the same Dracula we were taught to despise. And you, Sienna, have our father's affection. He tells us you've done only what you must to protect your friends. He said it was our actions that forced you to fight back."

"Well, your dad is right. He *wants* us to kill Samuel, though?"

"Our brother is a vampire," Alexander reminded us. "He's also followed a dark path. Our father hoped to redeem him, but Samuel chose power instead. We don't know what Samuel is planning, but we know he has figured out a way to enslave our father's ghost. Our father saw it coming and warned us. He told us to come to you. You'd know what we were talking about."

I glanced at Dracula and then at Delphine. "Do you think?"

"It's possible," Delphine allowed. "There's one spirit more powerful than the others. It could very well be Abraham."

Dracula nodded. "And we might not be dealing with the doctor possessing someone, but Samuel, who has taken the doctor's trinket. But how did Samuel Van Helsing learn of the trinket to begin with?"

Alexander cleared his throat. "I might be able to help with that. According to our father, he's been with you here for some time."

"What do you mean he's been *with* us?" I asked.

"With the dark power of the Scholomance, he's managed to take an inconspicuous form. Something you'd never suspect."

Dracula shook his head. "That damned rat. It's been Samuel Van Helsing all this time. Bats aren't the only creatures we can assume. A rat is little more than a wingless bat. To take that form, while not desirable, is certainly possible for one who has embraced the dark path of the Scholomance."

I clenched my fists. "So all this time, while we were screwing around with those ghosts at the asylum, Samuel was eavesdropping on us? He learned of the trinket and decided to make a play for it for himself?"

"I believe that's exactly what happened," Alexander confirmed. "Do not blame yourself for what has happened."

Dracula sighed. "Assigning blame is pointless. The fact of the matter is that we've given Samuel a chance to harness the power of his father. That's a ghost who wields the path of light combined with his path of darkness. There's no telling what they might accomplish together."

I groaned. "That's what *we're* supposed to be. The combined power of both, the power that mimics the Babylonian moon god, who emerges in darkness, but still reflects the light."

Dracula turned to the Van Helsings. "This is about more than saving your father. There's no telling what kind of hell Samuel might unleash on the world if he can wield the power of light through Abraham and the power of darkness himself."

I paced around the hall. "Well, we might have a way to stop

Samuel once and for all. We might need your help to find him and restrain him."

Alexander tilted his head. "Restrain him?'

I shrugged. "Beheading would do well enough. He has the same elixir you do, I presume, so there's only one way we can end him once and for all, and that's if my friend, the supernatural reaper, Zoey Grimm, can send his spirit to hell directly."

"She can't come here?" Alexander asked. "That would certainly be helpful."

I smiled. "She's indisposed at the moment. But if we can restrain Samuel and bring him to her, she can do the rest."

"And by restrain, you mean behead."

"Unless there's another kind of dismemberment you'd recommend that's just as effective."

Alexander looked resigned. "Nope. Beheading is certainly the best option."

"To behead my brother?" Reginald muttered. "I never thought I'd see the day."

I smiled, consciously exposing my fangs. "Don't sweat it. Just give me a clean shot and I can hit him from the astral plane. I just need you two to try to locate him and distract him so I can do my thing."

"He has control of his ghosts here," Dracula pointed out. "I suspect he intends to make a move against us sooner rather than later."

Dylan and his pack had been listening quietly all this time, but now he stepped up with Logan and Ian beside him. "We have one more full moon night this cycle. I say bring him on. We'll take him on together in the schoolhouse."

The Van Helsing brothers exchanged wide-eyed glances. "Are you sure that's a good idea?"

I smiled. "These wolves aren't bad guys. They can help."

"Now that Samuel has access to the dark path, a wolf's bite won't put him in a slumber," Dracula warned.

"But it will cause a distraction," I shot back. "Correct me if I'm wrong, but even with the power of the dark path, Samuel will have to consciously use his magic to resist the paralyzing effects of a bite. We just need to make sure he is here when the sun sets."

Alexander nodded. "We'll do what we can. I'm not sure how."

Dracula thought for a moment before he added, "We need to figure out if the doctor is truly here among the spirits. If not, we may need his assistance. If there's a way to dispel that trinket, or to overpower its influence on the spirits here, he'll know."

"Perhaps we can bid him to speak," Delphine suggested. "If he is here, we can try to offer him what he desires. If he is not, we can attempt to communicate with his spirit back at the asylum."

CHAPTER TWENTY

It took Delphine a while. The spirits in the schoolhouse weren't responsive. It made sense, though, that the ghost of Doctor Feuerhahn wasn't there. Samuel had lured the other spirits away from him and used the trinket to control them. Or perhaps he got the trinket first, then separated the patient spirits from their torturer. My guess was that he left the doctor behind because he didn't need the extra complication. Remove the doc from the equation, and ghosts trying to exact vengeance on one another wouldn't get in the way of his acquisition of the trinket, which he needed to take control of his father's ghost. All the other ghosts were pawns in his game, distractions to keep us off balance and thinking that he wasn't involved in the whole charade. Still, Dracula was right. The ghost of the doctor could come in handy, provided he'd be willing to talk. To make that happen, we'd have to offer him something solid. Literally. Like a solid, material body. A golem.

That was the ace in our back pocket. We weren't going to give the demented doc an invitation to retake corporeal form if we could get him to talk freely. Still, we had to be prepared for the possibility.

Morty retrieved an archeus crystal from the underworld. It was simpler than trying to recover the one I used before, which was still back in Kansas City with Zoey. Now that Morty's father, Azrael, had become a god and sat on the throne in the ethereal heavenly Olympus, getting a crystal like that wasn't difficult. Golems were what the gods used when they wanted to walk the earth in the flesh. The archeus crystals could be programmed through verbal commands. They usually required a likeness, an image, to replicate. We weren't especially concerned with giving the doctor a desirable body. I could easily look up some male models on my phone and give him a rather dashing figure. Instead, we used the photo of the doctor from the files Dracula stole to create the pattern for the crystal. It was a black-and-white image, so I had to speak a few commands to color him up. Giving him a body that was literally black-and-white would be creepy, to say the least. Not that the doctor didn't deserve the creepiest form we could make. I wasn't especially inclined to let him go on living in the golem after he helped us learn what we needed about the trinket. Then again, being bound to a body made him more manageable in some respects than he was as a vengeful spirit. It also meant he wouldn't be torturing those poor ghosts anymore. They wanted vengeance on him, and if they happened to get that opportunity, after he took a body, who was I to deny it to them?

Morty wasn't going with us to the asylum. He said he'd meet us back at the schoolhouse in about six hours.

We were almost certain that the doctor was left alone back at the asylum. The Van Helsings were off trying to track down Samuel. I didn't know what tactics they were using, but I did know they were good. After the Weird Sisters had compelled the wolves to attack Bourbon Street, the Van Helsing brothers had traced down every wolf in a matter of hours. They'd found Dylan and the other two wolves more than once, now. Somehow they'd tracked them far north of the city, made contact, and had a conversation. I suppose as old as they were, kept alive for more than a century by their immortality elixir, they'd had time to refine their tracking skills. Not to mention, they were Van Helsings. Tracking creepies and crawlies, fangs and ferals, was in their blood.

Delphine wrapped all her séance paraphernalia in a towel. She put it in the back of the van alongside our stash of swords, crossbows, and chain-mail armor.

The wolves rode in their own car. I wasn't sure what it was, but it looked old. The red paint was oxidized and it made strange noises when it ran. We'd all piled in the van in the past, but with all our stuff back there now, seat belts weren't an option.

Dracula rode shotgun. I knew the way to the asylum, but I had it on my van's built-in GPS just to be sure. Sneaking in in broad daylight wasn't going to be easy. The asylum was still a working mental hospital. We were interested in one abandoned and unused building. Dracula and I could get in easily enough. I could go astral or turn into a bat. Maybe. I still wasn't totally comfortable with the mechanics of that, but I was pretty sure I had the ability. Dracula could turn into a songbird or teleport himself past the fences and into or near the building. None of that mattered, though, because if this was going to work we had to *talk* to the doctor. We had to get Delphine into the asylum the old-fashioned way.

The only advantage we had was that there wasn't a thing in the old asylum that anyone would want to steal, and no one in their right mind would want to break into a place like that. Then again, there are paranormal researchers—a.k.a. geeks with cameras—who make a habit of seeking out haunted locations. For some reason, every time I turn to the Travel Channel, that's the theme. I suppose general travel didn't inspire a lot of creative content and dedicated audiences, so ghost-seeking shows became the prevailing theme. I'd watched a few. Most of the time, they didn't find anything conclusive, but they sure knew how to build anticipation.

For those television shows, capturing a ghost meant capturing it on *camera*. We were going for something more literal.

I could have loaned Delphine my brooch, which would allow her to get in while Drac and I flew over the fences. We still had to figure out how to get out of the place when we were done if the doctor was possessing a golem.

The old, abandoned asylum was on the perimeter toward the back of the property. There wasn't a clear drive that didn't pass in front of the newer and currently used buildings. The fences were designed more to keep patients *in* than keep people *out*. Still, fences tend to work the same way no matter what side of them you're on.

Dracula did a flyover of the property as a songbird so he could find a way in. When he came back to where we'd parked, he reported, "All right. There are no cameras along a stretch toward the back of the property. From there, we should be able to cut through the fence and get to the old asylum without anyone noticing."

I nodded. "All right. How do we get there?"

"Well, that's the thing. The reason there aren't any cameras on that side is probably because it's all marshland on the other side of the fence. We may have to get a little dirty to get through."

I shrugged. "I can still go astral."

"Hell no!" Delphine piped up. "If I'm getting my bottom-half soaked in swamp water, you're suffering with me."

I shook my head. "Nothing like a case of swamp ass to draw in the spirits."

Dracula snickered. "Sounds gh-ASS-tly to me!"

I shook my head. "And there's the joke. Right on cue."

"What did you expect?" Dracula pulled up his pant legs and waded into the swamp grounds around the perimeter of the asylum fence. "It was the butt of my joke!"

I glanced at Delphine. "See what I have to deal with? Butt jokes. All day long."

Delphine chuckled. "I raised three little boys. I'm used to it."

Dylan and the boys didn't complain much. They'd just returned from a night in the swamp, and they trounced through the muck like experienced pros.

Me, not so much. There's nothing nastier than the feeling of water and mud seeping through your shoes and between your toes. Wring those socks out later. Toe-jam tea, anybody?

I didn't like this tactic. I didn't like the fact that I had to suffer for no reason other than the fact that Delphine didn't think it was fair that she'd have to wade through the muck while I didn't. Well, you know what, shit ain't fair!

I kept my mouth shut. I was a team player on the outside, even if I was a whiny little bitch on the inside. Sometimes it pays to bite your tongue. Not something I'd recommend a vampire attempt. Metaphorically, it was a good idea. My fangs could get me into a lot of trouble. Not half as much as my tongue if I allowed it to wag at will.

We made it around to the rear of the property. The fence back there wasn't as fortified as the fences around the front of the property. Simple ten-foot chain-link fences topped with barbed wire. With a little vampire strength and the aid of my blade, I cut downward across the links. I made another cut parallel through the links a few feet over. It took a little tugging to free the bottom of the fencing from the weeds that had tangled through it over the years, but eventually I managed to pull it up. I hooked some of the bottom open links into the closed links above the opening. Just like that, we had a way in and out.

The sound of toes squishing in boots accompanied our short march from the fence line to the back of the old, abandoned asylum. Once we got back to the van, if anyone took their shoes off for the drive home, they might get a taste of my knuckles for lunch. Wet feet might be the second most disgusting smell in the universe, just under cat urine and comparable to wet werewolf.

Getting into the building itself wasn't a problem. We'd been there before. We didn't lock the doors behind us, and I'd have been surprised to find out anyone had been there since, other than Samuel Van Helsing.

We moved into the building. It was quiet and calm, nothing like the last time we were there. The building was still a mess. Poltergeists are like three-year-olds. Great at making messes, totally resistant to the notion of cleaning up after themselves.

We walked through the halls, and a door slammed upstairs. I almost jumped out of my skin.

"That wasn't a ghost," Delphine whispered. "Clearly a poltergeist."

Dracula nodded. "If Samuel took the patients away, he must've left some of the poltergeists manifested here behind. We'll have to be careful. Attempting to negotiate with the doctor's ghost might stir them up. Especially if the poltergeists were born in the psyches of those who were the victims of the doctor's experiments."

"Where do you want to do this?" I asked.

Delphine looked around. "The best place is somewhere central, in the middle of the facility. Ideally in an open and empty room. Something that doesn't have a lot of potential projectiles sitting around. If we stir up the poltergeists, we'd best minimize what ammunition they'll have at their disposal."

The asylum didn't have a central gathering area. It wasn't like modern-day homes with large recreational rooms. It felt more like a hybrid between a prison and a hospital than a facility dedicated to mental health. The wellbeing of the patients was hardly a priority in those days, at least for Doctor Feuerhahn. I didn't know much about psychology, though, and the theories for treating mental illness had surely made significant advantages since Feuerhahn's day. Combining lobotomies with electroconvulsive therapy might have seemed cutting edge in Feuerhahn's day, but even then, he surely knew the anguish he caused. He'd treated his patients more like lab rats than ill people who needed help.

"What about the doctor's office?" Dracula suggested.

"That's a possibility," Delphine agreed. "However, I suspect there's a lot of negative energy associated with that location. We're more likely to lure the doctor into a negotiation in a neutral room or location in the facility."

"Negative energy impacts his willingness to negotiate?" I asked.

"Think of it like how an emotional state of mind might impact your ability to carry on a rational, level-headed conversation with someone. If you're overwhelmed with anger or sadness, it's hard to open up and listen to reason. If you're more emotionally level-headed, you can think and hear more clearly. Spirits are more subject to the flux of emotions like anger, rage, or even embarrassment than living humans. Without the usual biochemical interactions that fuel emotions, spirits are easily swayed by the energy of their environments. Given all the horrors we know that have happened in Feuerhahn's office, trying to speak to him there would be like trying to flirt with a widow at her husband's funeral. The energy wouldn't befit the conversation."

"Got it. Is there anything you can do to neutralize the energy in a place?"

"I can, and I intend to do so. Such methods, though, are limited. The kind of energy that covers this place is intense and profound. More than I can neutralize with burning sage alone. We may find a place, ideally an internal room, with low energy. A place where someone hasn't died or where the doctor didn't conduct his experiments."

Dracula cleared his throat and pulled out a file folder from his cloak. I chuckled a little. He had been hauling that thing along all this time. He pulled out a sheet of paper that resembled a blueprint of the facility and showed it to Delphine. "I believe this room here was once a place where nurses congregated. A break room of a sort. I haven't seen anything in the records that would warrant a vengeful spirit directing his angst toward any of the nurses here. That might be as neutral a place as we can find, energy-wise."

"Good thinking," Delphine told him. "Let's give it a shot. I'll be able to get a read on the room pretty quickly."

Dracula led the way through the halls. The facility was a bit of a labyrinth, and it was easy to imagine getting lost there. It was enough to drive anyone crazy which, for a mental institution, was probably beneficial when it came to retaining their clientele.

Doors slammed, and we heard a few unidentified flying objects, probably of terrestrial origin, flying around elsewhere in the facility. Odd crashes, glass breaking, and a groan or two, made the whole experience unsettling.

We made our way to the break room. I had to admit, it was more peaceful than the rest of the place. The air was lighter. That I noticed it said something, considering my general lack of sensitivity when it came to paranormal phenomena. Even with my adoption by the Scholomance and my potential affinity to wield magic, I was no more psychic than a shoe. Probably less so. At least a shoe could predict a step ahead.

"Yes, yes," Delphine murmured. "The energy here is far more pleasant. This is the place."

"*Too* pleasant for the ghost of Doc Feuerhahn?" I asked.

Delphine shook her head. "The energy of a place impacts the disposition of a spirit, but it has no impact on the spirit's capacity to communicate or manifest. This location will serve our needs well."

Dracula and I stepped back, and Dylan approached me from behind and placed his hand on my shoulder. I still hadn't had a chance to tell him about all that had happened at the Scholomance. If I was on the path, I might be able to resist the paralyzing contagion that could impact me if he and I ever got frisky, or if our methods of protection failed. It meant we had a chance. Still, until I knew for sure how all this was going to pan out, I was trying not to think about it. We still had a tall order to fulfill before Dylan and I would have a real chance at romance. We had to end Samuel Van Helsing, and we had to fulfill the wishes of Sin and his priestess. We had to reunite the paths and become co-masters of a re-forged school of the moon.

I caught Dylan leaning in and taking a brief whiff of my hair. A little weird, right? But I liked Dylan. It was sweet.

We watched as Delphine laid out her summoning board and arranged her candles and various trinkets and crystals around the room. When she started lighting the candles, I knew the time had arrived.

"Shall we begin?" she asked.

Dracula nodded. "Are you prepared, Sienna? If he takes us up on our offer, he may require to see the golem that will become his new body."

I touched the bulge in my back pocket. "Yes, I have the crystal. It's programmed and ready to go. I just need a little light to channel through it and the crystal will create the golem we require."

"I can give you the light required."

I nodded. "All right, Delphine. Let's call the doctor. Is there anything you need from us to begin?"

"Calm your minds. Maintain a positive energy. Any negative thoughts can taint the energy of the room."

Like Peter Pan, I tried to focus on happy thoughts. I didn't think it would help me fly, but if it helped make the doctor more amenable to persuasion, then a little positive thought couldn't hurt.

CHAPTER TWENTY-ONE

I was thinking as positively as I could. I was good enough. I was smart enough. And, gosh darn it, people liked me. Stuart Smalley would be proud. It was hard to stay in that mindset since the mumbo jumbo coming from Delphine's lips was so strange. It vaguely resembled the "momma say" featured in Michael Jackson's *Wanna Be Startin' Somethin',* or "mecka lecka hi mecha hiney ho" from *Pee-wee's Playhouse.* As old-school as those references were, though, Delphine's chants were even older. I didn't know much about what traditions she'd relied on to master her craft. As I understood it, her abilities were inherited. I imagined the training and texts that guided her as she grew in power were also passed on from her ancestors.

The candles flared. The flames atop them were at least as tall as the candles themselves.

A semi-translucent figure appeared in the room. He had gray hair in tight curls. He was wearing a white coat and dark slacks. His ghostly form was mostly devoid of color, but his skin was pale and his eyes were black as night.

"I told you you'd soon become my newest patients," Doctor Feuerhahn greeted us.

"Not going to happen," Dracula fired back. "We're here to ask you a few questions."

Feuerhahn laughed. "Join my collection, and I'll answer all your questions."

I snorted. "Your collection? You refer to these people you killed as a *collection?*"

The doctor steepled his fingers and turned to me. "I liberated their souls from their disabled bodies and minds."

"And you enslaved the spirits here that you might continue to experiment upon them."

The doctor narrowed his eyes at me. "Psychology is a phenomenon of the mind, not merely the brain. The mind persists in some form even beyond death. Like this, the mind is without restraint. It is one thing to experiment upon minds contained within the body. It is another to experiment with minds in the wild, in their unrestrained form."

"What have you learned all these years?" Dracula asked.

"Very little. I was killed before my time. My dear patients were ungrateful and spiteful. They did not appreciate the gift!"

I rolled my eyes. "Gee. You stuck a metal rod in their heads and electrocuted their brains. I wonder why your name isn't the first thing they mention they're grateful for when they go around the Thanksgiving table in the afterlife."

Dracula raised his hand to silence me. I was getting a little mouthy, and an adversarial posture wasn't going to accomplish our purpose with the doctor.

"We've come to ask you about the strange trinket you possessed," Dracula said. "We believe it's come into the hand of someone else who has taken away your patients."

The doctor stroked his chin. "What you say is correct. Someone arrived here not long ago with the pendant you speak of. He stole my subjects."

"We need to know everything there is to know about that trinket," I demanded.

The doctor looked at me and grinned. "What's in it for me?"

I shrugged. "Maybe revenge on the guy who stole your 'subjects.'"

The doctor paced. He wasn't perfectly in sync with the physical world, and his feet hovered sometimes a half inch above and sometimes a half inch below the floorboards. He was creepy enough as it was, and none of this helped make our conversation more comfortable.

"Revenge against the thief will give me little consolation. The most it would do is leave me back in the condition I was before."

Dracula and I made eye contact.

"What if we could give you a new body?" I proposed.

The doctor smirked. "I've possessed a human or two in my time. It's not entirely pleasant. Their minds are never silent."

"But what if we could give you a body that's never been possessed by a soul, one without a previous mind or memories."

The doctor waved his hand through the air. "Impossible."

"Not impossible." I reached into my pocket and recovered the archeus crystal to hold in front of me. "This was made by the gods. It's how they create bodies for themselves when they walk the earth."

"I don't believe in anyone's gods!"

I shrugged. "What you believe doesn't determine if they do or don't exist. What I'm telling you is true. We can give you an unclaimed body."

"But you mustn't resume your experiments," Dracula warned. "The ghosts taken from here wish vengeance upon you. You will be powerless to thwart them without the trinket."

"Then get me my pendant!"

I chuckled. "This is a negotiation, ass hat. We aren't here as a charity organization catering to the desperate needs of psychopaths. We need the pendant. We need to know what it is, where you got it from, and how it works. The person who took it isn't exactly a saint. We have to stop him."

"If I tell you what you need to know, and you manage to retrieve my pendant, I get to have a body of my own?"

I nodded. "That's the deal. Once your information checks out."

"I'm no liar! I'll tell you the truth and tell you where to look to verify what I'm saying. You will give me my new body once I've given you the information. If you use that to secure the pendant or not is up to you. It is not my responsibility to ensure your success, which I could not do regardless as a ghost."

I exposed my fangs. "Accompany us in your new body and help us recover the pendant, and perhaps I won't make a snack out of you when all this is said and done."

Dracula raised one finger. "And if you make an effort to resume your efforts and kill anyone at all, I'll bite you myself."

Doctor Feuerhahn nodded. "Understood. I will have to find another reason to live, I suppose. But one needs to live before he discovers his purpose."

I smiled. "Stick to that philosophy, and we'll be cool."

"Then it's agreed. I will give you everything you must know about my pendant. After you give me my new body, I will accompany you as you attempt to recover it from the thief. After that, I will find other ventures to occupy my time."

"Ventures that don't include murdering people?" I asked.

The doctor rolled his eyes. "That's rich, coming from a vampire. Have you never killed for reasons less noble than mine?"

I clenched my fist. "I've only killed a couple of times, and it was to save my friends. Not to entertain my curiosities and explore my deluded theories."

The doctor folded his hands across his chest. "Very well. The terms are acceptable. The pendant you seek was once worn by a Babylonian priestess."

I tilted my head. "Ennigaldi?"

"Why, yes. How did you know?"

I sighed. "Just a guess."

"It cannot be a coincidence," Dracula mused. "Perhaps she meant for us to find it all the while. Maybe the idea to seek out the asylum was implanted in my mind without my recollection when I was last in the Scholomance."

I shook my head. "I have no clue. I agree. It's too strange a coincidence to be true."

"What are you talking about?" the doctor asked.

I waved my hand through the air. "None of your business. What can you tell us about how the pendant works?"

"It's simple. Whoever holds the pendant, no spirit can possess. No spirit can assault. And no spirit can disobey."

I nodded. "So it protects you from ghosts, but also gives you the ability to command them?"

"For a time," Doctor Feuerhahn agreed. "The problem is that it's impossible to know when its energy is expended. The moment the pendant is exhausted, the spirits are free. If you've used the pendant and violated a spirit's will, there's a good chance the spirit will come after you. As such, I only used the pendant sparingly and for short periods of time."

"That's why you had your office protected with salt."

The doctor nodded. "Of course. I needed a refuge where I could conduct my experiments without interference from the angry spirits in the asylum."

I shook my head. "I still don't understand. What were you trying to accomplish by these experiments?"

The doctor narrowed his eyes. "You wouldn't understand."

"Try me."

Feuerhahn took a deep breath. Ghosts didn't have to breathe, but neither did vampires. It was an old habit left over from our human days. "Insanity is a problem in the brain. The spirit exists apart from the brain. However, the mind can heal itself. By pulling spirits out of their bodies, if we could keep the bodies alive and increase the voltage of the electrical impulses within the brain at the same time, the spirit could theoretically use those impulses to fix his own mind."

"Fascinating. All your patients died, though. None of them fixed themselves."

The doctor bowed his head slightly. "The road to scientific progress is paved with failure. I'd have figured it out eventually."

"When those failures mean murdering people, you might want to reconsider your scientific ethics."

Doctor Feuerhahn shook his head. "Death has always been the vehicle of progress. Natural selection. The survival of the fittest. The weak must die that the strong might reproduce."

"Funny. A lot of vampires use that same notion to justify wiping out humans. Or, herding them like cattle."

"Perhaps they're correct. The point is when nature kills that a species might improve itself, we don't call it murder. When a doctor does it to the incurable, with the chance that it might lead to a breakthrough that heals them and millions of others forever, some call it murder. What's the difference if the end result is progress? Would you begrudge nature for elevating humanity from the apes?"

"Nature is impersonal. It doesn't make ethical decisions. We don't have that excuse."

Dracula cleared his throat. "Are we going to argue over the doctor's past, or are we going to get on with it?"

"I know what you're thinking," Doctor Feuerhahn said. "I've told you what you want to know. Why should you hold up your end of the bargain?"

I shrugged. "The thought did occur to me. But I stick to my word. You know, ethics and all. That shit matters."

"Pardon me for not taking a vampire's commitment to ethics seriously. If, however, you're considering not upholding your end of our deal, know this. The pendant can only be activated by a particular incantation. Without it, even if you recover it, it will be useless."

"Then tell us what it is!"

Feuerhahn laughed. "Once I have a body."

"How can we trust that you'll uphold your end of the deal?"

"I'm here with the most famous vampire in history, and another young vampire who is frightening enough in her own right. Not to mention, three werewolves are here. I'd be a fool to attempt to cut and run once I have a body. I'll give you the incantation. But not until you recover the pendant."

"Why not straight away?" Dracula asked.

The doctor shook his head. "The man who stole the pendant has a strange magic. He's manipulating its power somehow, activating the pendant by using a method I don't understand. You were right, before. I know you do not welcome me with open arms to your little team of monsters. But let's face it. We're all monsters, aren't we? I want to stop the man who took my pendant as much as you do."

"One more question," I said. "How did you acquire the pendant?"

"It was a fortuitous accident, I suppose," the doctor began. "My brother, may he rest in peace, was an archeologist. He discovered the pendant in a burial chamber in Ur. He had no family. He was killed when a tunnel he was excavating collapsed, and I inherited his personal wares. The pendant was among them, along with several notes on papyrus detailing how to use it."

"Do you still have those notes?"

Feuerhahn looked at me sideways. "I've been dead for nearly a century. Forgive me if I've lost track of my personal belongings. I cannot say if it remains with my heirs. What would they do with an old piece of papyrus written in a dead language? No matter, I remember everything. With or without it, I can help you learn to use it, without manipulating it through foreign magic. There's no telling how the pendant's properties might be warped when activated in ways it was never intended."

I looked at Dracula and then at Delphine. We all nodded in agreement. I didn't trust Feuerhahn any further than I could throw him, and since he was still a ghost, I couldn't throw him at all. I suspected he was making a play to get the pendant back for himself. We needed his help, though. I'd made deals with the devil before—Hades, in the past, and later, Athena—so if I had to work with a demented head-shrink, it was hardly the worst arrangement. Besides, I'd programmed his golem. It was an average body, filled with human blood. If he betrayed us, I could always use a fresh meal. Ever hear of meals on wheels? For vampires, it's lunch on legs. No one could argue that the doctor wouldn't deserve it. Especially if he betrayed us.

CHAPTER TWENTY-TWO

I held out the archeus crystal. Dracula stood beside me and extended his hand to cast a blast of pure white light into it. The crystal refracted the light and, picking up on the unique programming embedded into the crystal's structure, constructed a six-foot-tall golem in front of us. I'd made his hair darker than Feuerhahn's likely was when he died. I thought about doing a few things just out of spite, like giving him chronic back pain, a missing front tooth, a case of irritable bowel syndrome, or an itsy bitsy teeny weenie.

Instead, the only thing I did that might give him any problem was to make him gluten intolerant. I had to do *something*. The man was a monster who tortured and murdered his patients. The least I could do was deny him the pleasure of baked goods.

If he bitched about it later, I could always tell him it was an experiment. I did it in the name of science. I still had to come up with what the goals of that experiment might be, but you know, the road to progress comes with sacrifice, even if that sacrifice is only baguettes.

There's something unnerving about an unoccupied golem.

They could be programmed to do basic tasks, almost like robots. I'd made a few once for Zoey and myself back in Kansas City. Scantily clad men with well-defined mid-sections with cooking and cleaning protocols in their programming. When they weren't working, though, and they were standing there staring blank-faced into space, not even their washboard abs could compensate for the creepiness of it all. Mostly because they looked human. The kind you only see in magazines and movies, but human nonetheless.

Feuerhahn's golem wasn't attractive in the least. He wasn't ugly either. He was an average, somewhat geeky-looking man in his middle-to-late fifties. He looked as close to the original Quentin Feuerhahn as I could manage, given the limited photography available.

The doctor's ghost pushed his spectral form into the golem. It took a few moments before he moved. His legs wobbled beneath him. Thankfully, whatever mystical technology created the archeus crystal was able to produce material as well as flesh, and I'd made him a clothed golem. He was wearing a basic suit and wing-tipped leather shoes.

"Oh, my!" The doctor laughed at himself. "I forgot how *heavy* it feels to be in a body. I'd grown so accustomed to being a ghost!"

I shrugged. "I sort of know what you mean. I have the ability to walk the astral plane. You're right. Going back into the body can be a bit jarring even after a few minutes. I can't imagine doing so after a century as a ghost."

The doctor rubbed his stomach and smacked his lips. "I'm thirsty and hungry!"

"Sorry. Golems don't come with full stomachs. We can get you some McDonald's on the way home."

"What is Mcdonald's?"

I grinned. "You really didn't get out much at all as a ghost, did you?"

"Not at all!"

A loud bang sounded from one of the halls on the opposite side of the asylum. "How many poltergeists are we dealing with here?" Dracula asked.

Feuerhahn shrugged. "Not many. Maybe a dozen."

Delphine's jaw dropped. "A dozen poltergeists! Holy hell!"

Feuerhahn frowned. "Is that a lot? I wouldn't know. I don't have a lot of reference for that sort of thing. They're wily bastards. Most of them were brought about by my patients before they died. Before I died. They couldn't do much to me as a ghost, though."

"News flash, buddy. You're not a ghost anymore. They can hurt you now."

Feuerhahn gulped. "We need to get out of here."

I snickered. I can't say I was in a panic. The whole notion that the doctor had to suddenly run for his life from the poltergeists born from his patients' angst was what you might call just deserts.

Dracula, Delphine, and I led the charge. The doctor followed close behind while Dylan, Logan, and Ian pulled up the rear.

I wasn't sure how much our iron weapons would do to stop poltergeists. They don't come after you in a spectral form like ghosts might. They throw shit at you. Not literally. Unless a chimpanzee creates a poltergeist, I mean. But you get the point. Flying objects were the primary concern.

Until the floorboards under our feet shook.

"Does anyone else feel that?" I asked.

"We need to hurry," Dracula urged. "I think they're trying to take out the floors. Maybe the foundation of the whole place."

"Is a poltergeist strong enough to take out an entire building?"

Delphine shook her head. "One poltergeist, no. But twelve? It's possible. If we don't get out of here fast they're going to bring this whole place down on our heads. A hundred years of angst directed at a ghost they couldn't harm and now they have an opportunity. They're giving it everything they've got."

I glanced back at Feuerhahn. "Man, you must've really been a dick."

"No, I was never a detective. I was a psychiatrist."

I smirked. "Right. You don't know what a dick is. Doesn't mean it's not true. I mean, you are what you eat, right?"

"I don't follow."

Dylan was laughing. "I think she was calling you a cocksucker."

"Well, I'm no chicken. Though I do appreciate a good roasted leg and a thigh! That sounds delightful. I mentioned I'm hungry. I can get with your new-fangled lingo. In fact, I could go for some cocksucking right now! As soon as we get out of here!"

I clamped my hand over my mouth to restrain my laughter. We didn't have time for this. We took off across the asylum. Parts of the floor fell out behind us, and a few planks broke ahead of us. Some of the walls were cracking. Pieces of plaster crashed to the floor. Whatever glass was left in the place was shattered. In the hallways, we were clear of most of it, but a few shards flew out of the open doors of some of the patient rooms. One caught me in the cheek. It hurt, but it would heal over in a minute or two. Delphine tucked in with the doctor. They were the only two of us who could be hurt badly by things like that. So long as silver didn't go flying through the air, the wolves were fine. Dracula and I were more vulnerable. There was a chance that broken pieces of wood might come flying at us chest-height. We should have thrown on our chain mail before we came. Next time we were breaking the reincarnated ghost of a demented doctor out of a mental hospital where the ghosts of the patients and the poltergeists want him dead, we'd have to armor up.

The floor crashed down in front of us about four feet away from the front doors—our only escape. The wolves ran ahead and cleared the jump, no problem. Dracula and I could handle it.

Getting Delphine and the doc across was going to be more challenging.

Dracula and I stayed on one side. Delphine wasn't thrilled about the idea, but it was all we had. He grabbed her left arm and leg. I grabbed the right. The wolves waited with their arms open on the other side of the gap. We took three swings before tossing Delphine across the hole in the floor, where the wolves caught her. She looked a little rattled and somewhat surprised by the fact that she wasn't dead.

"All right, Doc. Your turn."

We picked him up the same way. We swung him back and forth three times to pick up momentum, but just as we released him, the floor under our feet gave way and we missed the mark.

The doctor was left hanging on the edge of the door sill. Dracula shifted into bird form before we hit the ground in the rubble below, and I touched my brooch just in time and went astral. It was a good thing, because a large broken board would have impaled me. I wasn't in the mood for impaling. If it hit my heart, bye-bye Sienna. If it missed, it would still hurt like a son of a bitch. I doubted I'd heal from *that* in a few minutes.

Using my astral form, I floated up to the surface as Dracula—back in his usual form—pulled Feuerhahn up and out of the building.

The entire building crashed down over me. Everyone else took off to avoid being struck by debris, and I remained in astral form until the building fell and I knew I was in the clear.

I touched my brooch when I was standing next to the doctor. "Boo!"

Feuerhahn nearly jumped out of his new body. He clutched at his chest. "Don't do that!"

I snickered. "I couldn't resist the chance to scare a ghost. Checked that one off my bucket list."

"You'd be surprised," Feuerhahn shot back. "Most ghosts are scared."

"Yeah, because you frighten the plasma right out of their ghostly little behinds."

"It's more than that. Imagine being in a world where you could see everything, but only occasionally make yourself known. Add to that the realization that this was all that was left for you until someone either came along and gave you a second chance with the reapers or your energy just faded out of existence."

I snorted. "Well, lucky you. Hey, Drac. Why do the assholes always get all the luck?"

Dracula smiled. "You're asking the wrong vampire. Major asshole for centuries, remember."

I nodded. "Right. See, that proves my point. You got lucky, too. Most assholes don't change. They just keep being assholes forever. All they have to give the world is shit. Sometimes a wide variety of shit, but shit no less. You didn't choose to give up your darkness, but it all worked out for the best."

"Perhaps it will work out as well for the doctor."

The doctor was already ahead of us with Delphine as they joined the wolves and squeezed past the fence and back to the marsh. "He tortured people, Drac. I don't know if he deserves a second chance."

Dracula cleared his throat. "Do you want me to tell each and every horrible thing I've done in my past?"

"That's different! You were changed on a mystical level."

"So has he. He has a new body, after all. What if there is something to his theory? What if whatever deranged illness he suffered from was a part of the brain rather than the mind? He has a new brain now. Maybe he'll be different this go-around."

"Well, aren't you the optimist."

"What can I say? I like to leave my victims half-full. Muaha-hahahaha!"

I grinned. He was laughing at his own joke, of course, but it wasn't a bad one. Not that he'd had any victims as of late. I couldn't quite say the same. And mine weren't left half-full or half-empty. They were empty. Perhaps that's where my pessimism over the doctor came from. Or maybe it was just common sense. Either way, I wasn't about to give him the benefit of the doubt. He had to earn it.

CHAPTER TWENTY-THREE

We stopped at Kentucky Fried Chicken on the way home. After all, the doctor said he had a craving for cock. Who was I to deny him? I was trying to coax him into using what he *thought* was the lingo for eating chicken among the "young folk" when he ordered, but Dracula and Delphine told him the truth and spoiled my fun. Freaking adults. I know, technically I was one, but just barely. It was harmless fun. So what if the doctor was embarrassed a little? He used to shove probes into people's brains and electrocute them. Now he was in a new body. He was like Frankenstein—the doctor and his monster all wrapped into one.

Of course, we needed him. That's why we were in this mess to begin with. The last thing we needed was to upset him or give him a reason to deceive us. In the end, whatever secret word unlocked his old pendant, we had to trust he'd give us the right one. How were we supposed to know the difference? Perhaps we'd use the word and, rather than give us control over the spirits, we'd speak the command that turned all of them against us. The doctor had told us that he intended to make us *his* patients, after all. Was Dracula so naive as to think that giving the old bloke a new body suddenly turned him into a saint?

If Dracula had a blind spot, it was that because he got a second chance and he changed, he thought everyone who used to be a serial killer deserved the same opportunity.

We ordered several buckets. A little bit of everything. Original. Extra Crispy. Everything but grilled. Delphine didn't have anything but coleslaw. The one thing I always pass up was the only thing she was eating.

The great thing about dining in at a fast-food joint is free drink refills. I don't know if they had soda pop back in the doctor's day, but the notion that he could fill his up over and over and select from a large variety of options was almost as exciting to him as an open vein was to me.

I didn't eat much. Chicken wasn't really my thing. Vampires *can* eat human food, but since we don't require it, well, *all* of it turns to waste. I'd learned the hard way a while back that it's best to keep my meals small. Use your powers of deduction to figure out why.

Feuerhahn downed a whole bucket himself. I lost count of how many biscuits he ate. I chuckled inwardly, thinking of the gluten intolerance I had snuck into his golem. He was on what must have been his third fountain drink. So far he'd tried a Coke, Sprite, and a Mountain Dew. He wanted to try all of them before we left.

The doctor was just finishing his drink. His straw gurgled in the bottom of his cup. His eyes widened.

"Oh, yeah. I forgot about that."

Feuerhahn took off across the restaurant and into the men's room. He came out a couple of minutes later. Did he wash his hands? Surely he hadn't forgotten the importance of personal hygiene, but, if he'd forgotten about urination there was no telling what other details about civilized living had skipped his mind during his century as a ghost.

"Amazing!" Feuerhahn was laughing as he returned to the table. "I completely forgot how good it feels to pee!"

I chuckled. "The thrills of living."

Dracula smiled widely. "I find it a bit of a pisser."

I stared at him blankly. "You might want to remove that joke from your repertoire."

"Sorry."

This little adventure was turning out to be more of a hassle than I anticipated. We needed Feuerhahn to tell us how to use the trinket. We were trusting the Van Helsing brothers to track down their brother so we could recover the trinket. Saving their father, Abraham, was their priority. If we could get the trinket, we could at least talk to Abraham via Delphine and learn exactly what Samuel was planning. If not, well, the only course of action was to behead him and take him to Zoey so she could reap his ass to hell.

Once again, we were off track. All the doctor wanted to do was enjoy the various associations of being alive again. I couldn't blame him, but we didn't have time to deal with all that. He'd had enough food. The wolves devoured a bucket each themselves. With a meal in Feuerhahn's golem belly and his lizard drained, we had no reason to linger. KFC wasn't exactly a great place to hang.

Morty was due to meet us back at the schoolhouse soon. He'd know if the trinket was anywhere nearby. We didn't know how the ghosts in the schoolhouse would react if we brought Feuerhahn in, but we had our iron. We could keep them off him if need be until Samuel showed. If it got too gnarly, Dracula could take Feuerhahn out for a drive and wait until it was time. I'd call him once we knew Samuel was nearby.

We hadn't originally anticipated that bringing Feuerhahn to the school in a golem would be a problem. Given the reaction of the poltergeists at the asylum, and that the spirits who created the poltergeists were in the schoolhouse, I was expecting the worst. The doctor said that the poltergeists were manifested by his patients *before* they died. Probably *while* he was experimenting on them. Dracula told me before that a ghost *could* create a poltergeist, but it wasn't common or likely. It would require an enormous amount of energy, and we barely had enough power running through the schoolhouse to keep the lights on and operate the booby traps.

I pulled Dracula aside as we piled back into our vehicles. I strongly encouraged Feuerhahn to ride with the wolves. It gave Dracula and me a chance to talk to Delphine on the drive back.

"I have an idea. I'll tell you on the way home. If the Van Helsings haven't caught Samuel yet, I think I know how we can draw him out."

CHAPTER TWENTY-FOUR

"You think if we stir up the ghosts by delivering Feuerhahn to them, it will lure Samuel back to the schoolhouse?"

I nodded. "He has them waiting there for something. If the pendant isn't there, there's only one thing that will motivate those spirits."

"Vengeance," Delphine guessed. "They'll come after Feuerhahn."

I squeezed my steering wheel. "We can protect him. If the ghosts got their vengeance, they'd be free. The reapers would come for them. Morty might be back already. That will help with the charade. If Samuel has a plan to use those spirits for some purpose, he won't want them to get their vengeance. Not until he's done with them."

"How do we know he's even watching?" Delphine asked.

"He hid in the walls as a rat before. I bet he's still there. His brothers wouldn't look for him there."

"You suspect he hid the trinket elsewhere?" Dracula asked.

"I don't think so. I just think it isn't active. Feuerhahn said he must be using some kind of magic to activate it, right? If he has to take control of the ghosts again, he'll turn on the trinket. When he does, we'll have to move fast. Morty will go astral, and I'll join him. We'll follow the signal and take him out."

"What about the Van Helsing brothers?"

"If they show up, let's hope they'll help if needed. They came to us for a reason. They know we have a way to send Samuel to hell. Hopefully Morty can portal us with Samuel's body to the underworld and from there to Zoey."

"Good thinking. I was anticipating a long drive with a decapitated Van Helsing in the back of the van."

I smiled. "I think we can avoid that. Besides, reaper portals get better gas mileage. Even better than my hybrid van."

"This plan will only work *if* Samuel is nearby. And if he believes using those ghosts is pivotal to his plan."

I glanced in the rearview mirror. "What do you think, Delphine?"

"I think it's the best plan we've had yet. It's not perfect, but we'll never know if it would work unless we try. What's the worst that could happen? If Samuel doesn't show, we fight off the ghosts and get the doctor out of there. We wait for the Van Helsings and we're back to the original plan."

Nothing is certain, I reflected. Especially when you're dealing with ghosts and enemies who've already shown themselves to be unpredictable. Samuel had not only fooled us when he made his move to become the president's sire and take over the world's governments, but he'd fooled the Weird Sisters who bought into his scheme and didn't see it coming when he practically fed them to us so we could take them off the table.

Maybe he didn't give a rat's ass—which at the moment was his own—about the ghosts he pulled from the asylum and dropped in our schoolhouse. Perhaps they were nothing but a distraction, a pain in the ass he planted to keep us off his scent. If so, all of this would prove pointless. Other than that, short of adopting a few dozen cats, we didn't have a good plan for stopping Samuel.

And even that wouldn't work if he wasn't still hiding in our walls in rat form.

We pulled up back at the schoolhouse. I pressed the button to open the side door of the van. Delphine climbed out of the back, and Dracula and I grabbed our iron swords again. If we had to protect the doctor, we'd need them. Not to mention, they might come in handy if Samuel showed his face. Then again, if he showed his face as a rat, the heel of my boot would do just as well. It wasn't likely he'd be that foolish. Especially not now that we were on to him. He was more than a pest in the walls gnawing on insulation.

Dylan, Logan, and Ian grabbed a couple of iron pokers.

"What about me?" Feuerhahn asked.

I shrugged. "Nothing to worry about." He didn't know that all the ghosts from the asylum were *in* the schoolhouse. At least I didn't think he did. "This is our home base. We won't let anything happen to you. Still, we're hoping to draw in Samuel, the guy we told you about who stole your trinket. We want to be prepared ourselves. We have a few extra bags of salt inside. If we run into a ghost problem, a handful of that should do the trick as well as anything made of iron."

Feuerhahn shuddered. "Yes. Salt. I remember. I used to use it often. Then I became a ghost."

"Don't worry," Dracula assured him. "We need you, remember? We won't let anything happen to you."

Feuerhahn cleared his throat. "Very well."

We went inside. It was always an ordeal coming and going. If we had a *normal* security system, we'd punch in the code and we'd be fine unless we missed a number and ran out of time. Our security system was more medieval and more deadly for supernatural threats of various stripes. Not too friendly to humans, either. Most things that can kill supernaturals, like stakes to the heart, silver bullets, and beheadings, also do the job on humans. Provided, of course, they aren't imbibing immortality elixirs.

Even then, the traps will stop them until they put themselves together again.

Once Dracula had the traps disarmed, we moved through and headed toward the old gymnasium. It was the biggest room in the old school and usually where we hung out. There, or the old cafeteria. Funny thing, though. I don't know how long that school had been closed, but the cafeteria *still* smelled of school lunches. I don't know if most people could smell it, but with my enhanced vampire senses, I did. It brought back visions of tater tots and square pizza.

At least the gym was mostly devoid of the odors typically associated with gym class. When I'd gone to Athena's hell and got to experience my "personal hell," it was exactly that—high school gym class. Since our group was devoid of competitive bitches, though, I didn't have much problem with the gym. It was a wide-open space that served our purposes well. If we were going to coax any ghosts (or a particular dirty rat) out of the woodwork, it was the place to be. It gave us plenty of space to maneuver if we had to start swinging swords and pokers.

I watched Delphine closely as we walked through the room. Her expression remained blank—nothing had triggered her sixth sense. I pulled her aside. "Are the ghosts gone?"

Delphine shook her head. "No, they're here. Spirits tend to be more active at night. Especially around the witching hour."

"Isn't that like three in the morning?"

Delphine shrugged. "That depends. Technically, the witching hour is between three and four in the morning. In my experience, any time after midnight is primed for supernatural activity."

"Why is that?" I asked.

"There are theories. Just because I can speak to ghosts doesn't mean I know all the ins-and-outs about how they work. Some believe that ghosts are active all the time and we only tend to see them more when it's dark and the lights are out. Personally, I think it has something to do with the moon."

"Sort of like how the full moon can affect werewolves?"

Delphine nodded. "Perhaps. Just as likely, it's how the moon affects gravitational forces as reflected in the rising tides. It could be something different altogether."

I pressed my lips together. "I wonder if it's connected to the kind of force I learned about at the Scholomance. The unification of light and dark sources of magic."

"It's possible. Ultimately, these are vengeful spirits. Even though Feuerhahn is here, they might not recognize him. Or, they're biding their time. Gathering enough energy to make sure their attack is effective."

I sighed. "If we have to wait until night, the wolves will shift. They might be fine here, but they need room to run. They tend to get restless if kept indoors under a full moon. While I don't think Dylan would do anything horrible, he certainly won't *want* to stay inside under a full moon. It's like asking a fish to hang out on a dock. Every instinct it has tells it to flop around until it lands back in the water."

"There are still a lot of werewolf hunters in the city." Dylan had walked up behind me and rested his hand on my waist. "Sorry, wolf hearing. I figured I could add my two cents to the conversation."

I nodded. "Not all the hunters are in league with the Van Helsings. If you guys shift in the gym, do you think you'll be able to resist the urge to take off out onto the streets?"

"Honestly? Probably not. I hate to say it. When we're wolves, instinct is primary. We still have some degree of rational thought, but it's drowned beneath a sea of pheromones and instincts that makes it hard to resist our primal urges."

"You don't kill, though. Not usually."

"Right. That's a myth about werewolves. As you know, in feudal times, we were once the protectors of villages against bloodthirsty vampires. Even now, we don't usually attack humans unless provoked."

"And if you are provoked?" Delphine asked.

"Then we fight back or we run. Fight or flight. It's as primal a survival instinct for werewolves as with any creature, including humans. There are exceptions, of course."

"What kind of exceptions?"

Dylan shrugged. "Rogue wolves. Humans have psychopaths and serial killers. Our kind isn't without its share of those who give the rest of us a bad name."

"Our plan is to try and coax out the ghosts. We think they'll go after the doctor for vengeance which, in turn, might lure Samuel out to retake control."

Dylan nodded. "Well, if you can't do it before nightfall, we'll do our best to restrain ourselves. If Samuel shows, it's all hands, and paws, on deck."

"Are you sure you can keep Logan and Ian under control?"

Dylan smiled. "They won't be a problem. They'll feel all the urges I do, but I can rein them in if they attempt to leave the school."

"All right. Well, anything we can do to speed this along?"

Delphine shrugged. "I don't know how much control you have over this magic you got from the Scholomance."

"Not much. I'm not really sure how to make it work. Back in the void, it was easy. I'm not sure I've fully grasped it yet in the flesh. I might not until this is done."

"Then Dracula might be able to release some of his energy into the air. Anything that the spirits can draw on to manifest will help."

"Doing that without spooking the doctor is the challenge," I said. "He agreed to help us acquire the pendant. I'm not sure he would have if he knew it meant using him as ghost bait."

"Spirits can draw on any kind of energy," Delphine explained. "Magic is especially potent, but heat and electricity will also do. Turn up the thermostat. Flip on as many lights as you can. Spirits can absorb quite a bit and save it up until they're ready. They still might not use it all until nightfall, but at least it will improve the chances that they manifest then."

"Sounds good. Morty should be here any second. I'm going to check my room. That's usually where he appears. Try to keep everyone entertained, especially the doctor. Don't let him out of your sight. We don't want him wandering off alone. I still don't trust him. If I was in his shoes, I'd cut and run the first chance I had."

Dylan nodded grimly. "If he tries anything, he won't get far."

CHAPTER TWENTY-FIVE

It took a lot of energy to heat the schoolhouse, so we didn't run the furnace often. It was an old boiler system that smelled when we turned it on, and radiators were at the perimeters of every room. I wasn't sure how efficient it was. Probably not very. But if we could raise the temperature in the place a few degrees, it might help draw the spirits out. I also flipped on all the lights between the gym and my room.

While we were in the gym, talking about the plan wasn't a huge problem. If Samuel was hiding as a rat he was probably in the walls somewhere. In the wide-open gym, he probably couldn't hear us so long as we kept our voices down. Vampires have good hearing, but I knew from my time as a bat in the void that my usual senses gave way to what was natural to the form I assumed. If that held true in the real world, Samuel couldn't hear us any better than any rat might.

I returned to my room and was surprised to see Morty sitting on my bed, his shoes and socks off, clipping away at his toenails.

"What the hell are you doing?"

Morty stared at me blankly.

Snip.

I watched as a nail clipping went flying across my bedspread. "What does it look like?"

"You're clipping your nails on my bed?"

Morty shrugged. "It's more comfortable than doing it on the floor."

"You dress like a dandy, but you're an animal. Do you know how gross that is?"

"I'll collect the clippings when I'm done."

I bit my lip. "You're here to help me, so I'm going to *pretend* I'm not thoroughly disgusted by you right now."

"They're toenails. Everyone has them." Morty grinned and slipped his sock back on.

"How long have you been here waiting?"

"Not long. Maybe an hour."

"And you happened to have nail clippers in your cloak?"

Morty tossed me the clippers he was using. "Sorry."

"These are mine!"

"Look, you and Zoey are practically sisters. That means we're family."

"No, it doesn't."

Morty winced. "Sorry. I'm not good with boundaries."

"Have you sensed the trinket at all since you arrived?"

Morty shook his head. "Not once. Do you have a plan?"

I nodded. "I don't want to talk about it here. We're too close to the walls. There's no way to know if Samuel is listening in. I'm just glad you're here. If everything goes as intended, we might need your portaling services."

Morty smiled and nodded. "Got it. Don't say too much. I can put the pieces together."

It occurred to me that if Samuel was listening in, I could use it as an opportunity to lure him in. "Just make sure you have reapers ready. The ghosts here have a vendetta to settle and the object of their vengeance is with us."

Morty raised an eyebrow. "You brought the doctor? Did the archeus crystal work?"

"He's here and in the flesh. We might not be able to stop Samuel since we don't know what he's planning, but at least we can give some restless spirits a long-overdue chance to move on."

I winked at Morty when I finished speaking, hoping he'd get the hint.

Morty smirked. He figured it out. "Got it. I'll have some reapers ready to collect them. Let me just hop back to my office and I'll tell Carmilla to get everything ready."

"Sounds good. Be back shortly?"

"It'll take five minutes. Ten, tops."

"Great. I'm trying to put some energy into the air. Heat, electricity, whatever. Anything that'll help the spirits manifest."

"I can help with that when I get back. When the Grim Reaper whips it out, all the ghosts go wild."

"You're talking about your scythe right now, I assume."

Morty grinned. "Am I?"

I laughed. "You're horrible. Meet us back in the gym."

CHAPTER TWENTY-SIX

Hopefully, Morty was right. If whipping out his rod and scythe could stir up some of the spectral slackers, we might be able to get this thing done before Dylan and company wolfed out.

We'd lived in the schoolhouse for months. Even before the place was infested with ghosts, it was mildly creepy to walk the halls alone. Given all the adolescent angst that once filled those classrooms and halls, it was a wonder that we didn't have a few poltergeists of our own. Now that we had the ghosts of mental patients there along with the rat form of a vampiric Van Helsing spying on us, it was even more unsettling walking alone across the school. Nothing bad had ever happened but, you know, imagination is a powerful thing.

Something funny happens when you're expecting something bad to happen. You start *almost* seeing things. Shadows on the wall. A bug flying somewhere in your peripheral vision. The brain takes those minor inputs and makes you think, even if only for a split-second, that it's more than it is.

Enough false alarms and your brain starts to give you that "little boy who cried wolf" effect. You can only be falsely spooked so many times before you get a little numb to it. I was still on edge, but if something did happen, I was just as likely to dismiss it as my mind playing tricks on me. The same principle applied to sounds. Every little sound made me wonder if it was Samuel scratching in the walls. Unless one of his abilities was to replicate himself, though, it couldn't be him. The strange sounds that came from the schoolhouse were all over. He was a rat, but it didn't mean he was the only one. There were mice there, too. I didn't see many of them but there was only one explanation for the mysterious collections of black rice that showed up in various places and returned days after I cleaned them up.

I made it back to the gymnasium without any notable incidents. The three werewolves, Feuerhahn, and Delphine were sitting in a circle. Dracula was walking around the outside, patting each of them on the head.

"Duck. Duck. Duck. *Goose!*"

Dylan got up and ran behind Dracula.

Dracula saw me and stopped running. "We're having fun. Pleasure releases energy too, you know."

"This is good fun!" Feuerhahn added. "I wish I'd heard about this game when I was younger. Come to think of it, my body is only a few hours old. I'm practically a child again!"

I scratched my head. If someone had told me a couple of years ago that I'd eventually find myself in a room seeing Dracula play Duck Duck Goose with three werewolves, a medium, and a ghost possessing a golem, I would have asked what the punchline was. Seeing it with my own eyes, I realized there was no punchline. The entire scene was the joke. If I hadn't walked into the room already on edge, obsessing over my plan, I might have even laughed. It took me off guard.

That was one thing I'd learned several times over now about Dracula. No matter what the situation, no matter how grim or important the issue at hand, he had a way of *not* taking it especially seriously. In some instances, I suppose, it was a good character trait. Anxiety and tension can be a distraction. Staying carefree and loose can be a good thing. It can also leave you ill-prepared for what's coming.

"Morty will be here soon. He thinks he can stir up the spirits. We might be able to move up the timetable a bit on our plans."

Dracula nodded. "Good thing we sent some positive vibes into the atmosphere. Good energy should take the edge off."

"They're vengeful spirits. Can you really take that edge off with good juju?"

"Actually, yes," Delphine said. "You're right. Vengeful spirits will seek retribution against their target. A little positivity in the air makes it less likely that they'll leave much collateral damage behind."

"Like hurting other people?"

"Exactly."

"I'm sorry," Feuerhahn broke in. "What are you talking about? You're calling out the ghosts now?"

I bit the inside of my cheek. We hadn't shared with him all of our plans. "Don't worry. We've got this figured out. Mostly."

Feuerhahn nodded. "I'm sure you do."

"Was that a vote of confidence?"

Feuerhahn stroked his chin. "You fashioned this body from a crystal. It's remarkable. This body is far more vigorous than my former one. If you could pull this off, I have no reason to suspect you don't know what you're doing. Besides, we had a deal. When this is done, provided I don't hurt anyone or resume my experiments, I can get about starting a new life."

I narrowed my eyes. "I'm not sure we finalized the details of that deal, but I'm not opposed to it. If this works out, and you can keep your whole murder-for-the-sake-of-progress schtick in the past, then fine."

"Deal." Feuerhahn extended his hand. I shook it. It was unsettling. His hand was as soft as a newborn baby's, but the size of a grown man's. I don't *like* callouses on a man's hands, mostly because I don't find exfoliation an enjoyable form of foreplay. If a man's hands are *too* soft, well, that's equally disturbing. I don't know why, exactly. I can't explain it. But I think most ladies out there would agree. There's something about a man with silky-smooth hands that says he can't be trusted. In Feuerhahn's case, the tenderness of his skin was pretty far down the list of reasons why I didn't trust him, but it fit my overall impression that he was an irredeemable scoundrel.

When Morty returned, he was in his cloak. He had clearly picked up on the significance of my wink. The cloak was the official uniform for a reaper preparing to harvest souls. If we were going to sell the plan and lure Samuel out, the cloak would help.

Dracula stepped over to make eye contact with Morty and nodded. "Good to see you, Mortimer."

Morty nodded. "There are souls here soon to be released from their vengeance. I'm here to collect them."

Dracula looked at me. I winked at him the same way I did at Morty before. I wasn't sure if Dracula would pick it up. He wasn't as savvy when it came to picking up non-verbal cues as Morty was, but thankfully he got the hint. "Good to hear. It's high time that these troubled souls will have a chance to rest in peace."

Morty stepped into the middle of the gym floor, at what was once half-court on the basketball court. He swung his scythe overhead. It radiated a faint golden glow, but once he harnessed souls, the glow would brighten until it was almost blinding. There's a lot of power in souls.

"The souls are stirring," Delphine murmured. "I'm not sure it's enough."

"May I attempt something?" Feuerhahn asked. "I've been a ghost for a long time. Besides, it's me they want. I might be able to coax them out."

"Are you sure?" I asked. "Those ghosts are going to swarm you the first chance they get."

Feuerhahn nodded. "I should be fine. Can I borrow your sword in case?"

I bit my lip and looked at Dracula. He nodded. How much damage could the doctor do with an iron sword? It couldn't kill vampires or werewolves, and I could defend Delphine if push came to shove.

I reluctantly handed my sword to Feuerhahn. "Don't get any funny ideas."

"I wouldn't dream of it," he assured me.

Feuerhahn looked around the room and fixed his eyes on one of the far walls, just behind where the basketball hoops would have been.

Feuerhahn approached the wall and thrust his fist into the plaster, leaving a hole.

"*Dalamu!*" Feuerhahn shouted.

No sooner did he say it than Morty stopped swinging his scythe. "I can feel it!"

A black rat crawled out of the hole. Feuerhahn extended his hand and pointed at the rat. Its shape expanded until Samuel Van Helsing—still wearing the suit he wore when we left him in the void with his father—was there with wide, illuminated eyes.

All at once, several glowing spirits appeared. I counted them out. Seven in total. They were glowing white, and half their forms resembled the upper halves of human bodies, with bottom halves that were less defined, like wispy tails following behind them.

I ran over toward the doctor. He extended one hand, and a black power blasted from his palm and struck me in the chest. After it hit me, it formed a barrier that separated us from the doctor and Samuel.

The spirits passed through it with no problem, but we couldn't break through.

Dracula blasted it with light. Feuerhahn held his hand steady to resist Dracula's power.

"What the hell is he doing?" I shouted. "He's wielding the power of the Scholomance! How is this possible?"

The ghosts shot at Samuel Van Helsing like darts penetrating his chest. Once they had disappeared inside him, Feuerhahn swung my iron sword and lopped off Samuel's head, then smashed it with his foot.

The spirits floated out and over Samuel's body. Only now, there were eight. Seven of them were white and floated peacefully. The eighth was red.

"They need to be reaped," Morty said. "All of them."

"You can't reap Van Helsing," I reminded him. "He's a vampire. We need Zoey for that."

Morty shook his head. "That's not Samuel. The spirit that was in Van Helsing's body was the doctor."

"Then who was that in the golem?"

Dracula groaned. "It's Samuel Van Helsing. He deceived us! He took the place of the doctor all this time!"

"What the hell? He looked just like the picture of the doctor!"

Delphine sighed. "Spirits can appear in whatever form they like. They just most commonly choose to take the form that resembles their former selves."

The real Samuel Van Helsing turned. "I think I'll be leaving now. Thanks for the cure."

"The what?" I asked.

Someone behind me answered, "The cure for our brother's vampirism."

I turned and saw Alexander and Reginald. Alexander held a crossbow in his hand—perfect for staking. Reginald held a rifle, presumably loaded with silver bullets.

"You'll allow our brother to leave with us," Alexander growled. "Or we'll take all of you out one by one."

Samuel, in the golem I'd made for him, bent over and took the pendant off his former body and placed it around his new neck. He walked toward us. "You'd best take my brothers seriously. They're crack shots, the both of them."

"Then why don't they shoot us?"

Samuel narrowed his eyes. "Consider it an act of mercy, and my thanks for the new body. I'm human again. No longer an abomination like you."

Morty took off after the freed spirits, swinging his scythe. He was gathering them one by one.

"You're going to allow us to live out of *gratitude?*" Dracula asked. "I don't believe that for one second."

Samuel shrugged. "Perhaps you'll be useful later."

"What are you going to do?" I asked. "You're not a vampire anymore. You can't manipulate the president as before. Your sire bond won't hold."

Samuel clutched at his gut as he laughed. "My plans are much bigger than that."

Dracula, Delphine, and I stepped back as Samuel walked past us. I wasn't sure we could take him down if we tried. If I went astral, the Van Helsing brothers would open fire.

"Alexander!" Dracula shouted. "How did you two get past my traps?"

Alexander laughed. "There's one spirit not yet accounted for, isn't there?"

Dracula sighed. "Abraham."

Alexander nodded. "All he wanted was to cure our brother. Now that Samuel is human again, I imagine he'll be at peace."

I shook my head. "Samuel was his tether?"

The Van Helsing brothers smiled as Samuel joined them. Alexander reached into his pocket and handed Samuel a small vial. I didn't need to ask what it was. It was their immortality elixir. Samuel downed it in one swallow, and the three brothers turned to leave the gymnasium.

Samuel stopped before he passed through the double doors to remove the pendant and throw it at me.

I reached up and caught it. "What is this? You're giving it up?"

Samuel shrugged. "I don't need it anymore. Remember, Sienna. There are still three ghosts possessing three men. They won't be too thrilled to find out I took the trinket. You can use it to force the spirits from their bodies. Good luck. I hope you remember the magic word."

I snorted. "Yeah, I heard what you said. Ass."

Samuel left and followed his brothers out the door.

Morty stepped up beside us. "Well, I don't know if we should call that a victory or not. But at least these poor spirits can finally be put to rest."

I shook my head. "I can't believe it was Samuel's spirit, separate from his body all this time. We put him in that golem while that doctor's ghost was here with the others all the while."

"Don't beat yourself up over it," Delphine consoled me. "I couldn't tell the difference, either."

"The dark path of the Scholomance is powerful," Dracula said. "I'm the one who should have seen it coming."

I took a deep breath. "Ennigaldi said I had to kill Samuel."

Dracula nodded. "Perhaps we'll get our shot another time. When we don't have bolts aimed at our hearts. Morty's right, though. This wasn't a total loss."

"They could have *killed* us," I reminded him. "Samuel said we might still be useful. What the hell did he mean by that?"

Dracula sighed. "Your guess is as good as mine."

CHAPTER TWENTY-SEVEN

Now that Samuel was in a human body, Zoey was off the hook for his reaping. All we had to do was behead the bastard and sledge-o-matic his head like a watermelon. That wouldn't be easy. His brothers and the ghost of his dead father were watching his back, and he wielded the dark power of the Scholomance.

That wasn't what I was most worried about. He *gave* us the damned trinket back. It was almost like he wanted us to use it. I remembered the magic word: *dalamu*. I didn't have a clue what it meant, of course. Was it ancient Babylonian? Did Babylonians actually speak a language called Babylonian? Google told me it was Akkadian.

I was a computer chick, sure, but I was no linguist. Dracula didn't know what it meant. Delphine didn't have a clue, either. Morty was at a loss as much as the rest of us.

The best shot we had at understanding the pendant and what it *really* did was to go back and hope we'd find MGD. The good news was that, with the doctor gone, if they left their bodies they'd be free to move on. No more tethers. Would they be willing to do that? One of them had held on to the doctor's trinket for years. If anyone knew what it did, or how the doctor came into possession of it, it was them.

Everything that Samuel, masquerading as Feuerhahn, told us was crap. All of that still left the question: how did a demented psychiatrist acquire a Babylonian relic? Could it really be a coincidence that the same ghosts Dracula had us hunting just happened to hold a relic that corresponded with the deity who'd appeared to me in the Scholomance? Was it possible that something was implanted in Dracula's mind when he entered the path of light? Possibly, but when I was talking to Ennigaldi, she said that she and Sin moved to the Scholomance when Samuel Van Helsing arrived. That was *after* Dracula mastered the path of light. Then again, if the two paths of the Scholomance were once united in the lunar power of Sin, it wasn't impossible that something about the power of light drew Dracula to the asylum on a subconscious level. One thing I knew for sure—this was all connected, somehow.

Morty suggested sending me back to the Scholomance. We could ask Athena, even some of the Olympian gods, if they knew something about the pendant. I wasn't sure that I'd get a response in the Scholomance, though.

We decided to divide and conquer. Morty took a photograph of the pendant to take to Olympus and show to his father. He'd find out what he could about it. Meanwhile, Dracula, Delphine, and I planned to go back to the Garden District. We still had a few hours before we had to worry about sunset and the wolves. Dylan wasn't a hundred percent sure that they'd shift. It wasn't consistent. Sometimes they shifted on three consecutive nights during a full moon, other times it was only two.

Morty decided to do his best to keep them contained in the schoolhouse. Now that Samuel wasn't a rat in our walls—or rather, the demented doctor wasn't trapped in Samuel's rat form in our walls—no one would be there to disturb our salt barriers. Dracula could reset the traps and protect them so that Abraham, if he was still helping his sons, couldn't cross and trigger the traps. A ghost with the power that Abraham wielded might be able to produce a gust of wind and blow the salt away, but the best we could do was the best we could do.

I hoped we'd be back from the Garden District before the wolves were an issue. Worst-case scenario, we could stand guard outside of the school just to make sure the wolves didn't lose control. It would be a long night, but with so much unknown about what the Van Helsing brothers were planning, sending them off to a random swamp wasn't a viable option. The brothers had tracked them hours north of the city before. There wasn't anywhere they could go that the Van Helsings couldn't track them again. As big of a pain in the ass as they were, I had to admit that their tracking skills impressed me.

Dracula, Delphine, and I returned to the Garden District in my Toyota Sienna. The last time we'd gone there, we hadn't found any of the ghost-possessed we were looking for. Maybe Samuel scared them off. We could only hope they'd be back home.

Before we left, Dracula needed to reset the traps. He could disable them easily enough if we were coming and going per usual. After the traps were triggered, though, more darts had to be put into air-powered shafts, more fuel had to be added to flame throwers, and the blades that spun out from the walls had to be retracted. It was an ordeal.

Even more so when they kept getting re-triggered the second he set them.

"What in bloody hell?"

I tilted my head. "Maybe there's something wrong with the mechanism."

Dracula shook his head. "It's wrong with all the mechanisms then. They're all doing this."

"Delphine, are there any ghosts left here?"

Delphine frowned and placed her fingers to her temples to focus. "Not any ghosts…"

I heard a loud bang from somewhere back inside the school. We took off in the direction of the sound. In a large building like that, it's hard to know *exactly* where a sound originated. If it didn't happen again, we'd probably never figure it out unless we spotted something out of place. That didn't stop us from chasing the noise.

I was hauling ass down the hall when a gray figure appeared and shot straight through me. I didn't see a face before it struck. When it hit me it pulled the air right out of me. I fell to my knees and clutched my chest. "Son of a bitch!"

"Are you all right?" Dracula asked.

I gasped for air. "Yeah. Will be. What the hell was that?"

"Looked like a ghost. I thought Morty got them all."

Delphine shook her head. "Not a ghost. I'd know it if it was. That was a poltergeist."

I coughed in my hand as I got back to my feet. "A poltergeist? I thought we didn't have any of those here?"

"It's powerful," Delphine said. "It looks like it's new. Created by someone in angst. More than that, there's more power behind it than usual. Poltergeists rarely appear like that. They're like the wind. You see the effects, but never the entities themselves."

I shook my head. "I don't understand why the hell we have a poltergeist. We gave all those spirits a release. They got their vengeance."

"Could it have been the doctor?" Dracula asked.

"For a ghost to produce a poltergeist like that, he'd need a lot of power," Delphine explained. "Feuerhahn has been dead a long time. I don't think even with all the energy we put into the air he could have created one like that. It's also not often intentional. It follows and manifests in ways that reflect the angst of the one who cast it."

Dracula pinched his chin. "Van Helsing."

"Which one?"

"Abraham. We knew he was here. We also know his ghost triggered the traps to let the brothers through."

I scratched the back of my head. "That doesn't make sense. The brothers claimed they wanted us to free him from Samuel's control, but then we found out that curing Samuel of his vampirism was the endgame. They said it put him at peace."

"Something made him upset," Dracula guessed.

"More than upset," Delphine added. "Poltergeists don't just manifest when you've had a bad day. It takes intense anguish and anxiety. There's something about what was going on here that he didn't like."

"Then why give us the trinket? If they pissed him off somehow, you'd think they'd want to keep him under control."

Dracula shook his head. "This whole damn ordeal has been like peeling an onion. Each layer more bitter than the last."

I patted Drac on the back. "If it makes you cry, that's okay."

"Dracula doesn't cry."

I rolled my eyes. "Sure you don't. I'm with you, though. Every time we solve one clue as to what's going on, it only opens up a bigger mystery. You'd think we were in a damned Agatha Christie novel."

Dracula shrugged. "Or one of those cozies with cartoon cats and witches on the cover."

This was new. "You read *cozy* mysteries?"

"Cozy *paranormals*, thank you very much. What did you expect I'd read?"

"I don't know. Horror, maybe?"

"Pfft. I can't read that stuff. I prefer speculative fiction. That realistic stuff is too boring."

I chuckled and shook my head. Only Count Dracula would hate horror because of its realism. Given his history, a good fright was just another day at the office. The one thing about most horror, though, is that it's more predictable than other speculative genres. Certainly more predictable than mysteries. Perhaps once this was all said and done, those cozies would be too realistic for him. I found nothing about this situation remotely cozy. Since "annoying as fuck mysteries" wasn't a category you could browse on Amazon, hopefully this predicament wouldn't entirely spoil his reading choices.

CHAPTER TWENTY-EIGHT

There wasn't anything we could discern about the poltergeist. Whatever angst Abraham Van Helsing experienced when he birthed it, it wasn't violent. He wasn't going after us. If anything, it kept disarming the traps. Every time we headed for the door, it picked up again. It was almost as if Abraham's poltergeist was trying to keep us inside. Poltergeists don't have well-rounded personalities. They have a single mood. They aren't logical. They act from a distinct motive bound to their maker's angst. Was Van Helsing trying to stop us from doing something? Was he trying to help us, or was he pissed that his sons finally had a chance to take down the infamous Dracula and passed up on the opportunity? If that was the case, one would think the poltergeist would be more violent. Like the ones at the asylum, shaking the walls, rattling the building until it crashed down almost on top of us.

"I don't think this thing wants us to leave." I stared down the hall waiting for another bang.

"Perhaps it knows what we're going to do," Dracula suggested. "It may be that Abraham doesn't *want* us to learn the truth about the pendant before we use it. I wouldn't put it past him to have a far more insidious plan in his ethereal back pocket than Samuel."

"Have you ever sat down and had a serious conversation with Abraham?" I asked.

Dracula huffed. "Of course. Between all the times he tried to shove a stake into my heart, we decided to chat about Transylvanian weather in the summertime. Of course we don't *talk*. We're mortal enemies. Always have been."

"You *were* mortal enemies, Drac. Unlike you, while you were off mastering the path of light, I was stuck in the Scholomance with his ghost. He's not an evil man. He hated you for the same reasons you hate who you used to be. You and he aren't all that unalike."

Dracula folded his arms in front of his chest. "You're right. He wasn't a bad man. He was closed-minded, bigoted, and naive, though."

"Bigoted?"

"He hated all vampires!"

"Or did he only hate the vampires who were like you used to be? You know, the ones who fed on innocent maidens in their sleep and terrorized poor Jonathan Harker."

"He wanted his own son to change. He convinced his other sons to deceive us into arranging for a golem to make it happen."

I shook my head. "Did he? The golem was *our* idea."

"One we talked about here in this schoolhouse," Delphine reminded me. "Where Samuel was listening in. He saw an opportunity to shed his vampiric body and took us up on it."

"I'm not sure why he'd do that," Dracula argued. "Isn't the power of the Scholomance especially suited for vampires? Didn't you say, Sienna, that the Babylonian god wanted us to be his knights of the night to defend the world against greater evils like demons and such?"

"I did. But humans, like Abraham, have embraced the paths of the Scholomance as well. Perhaps rejecting his vampirism was a part of his effort to reject what Ennigaldi told me we were made to do."

Delphine shook her head. "You two could go round and round about this until the moon rises and the wolves get hairy. Are we going to go see Mitchell, Garret, and Daniel, or not?"

I nodded. "Poltergeist's warnings or not, we have no way of knowing what it means. We're going."

No sooner did I say it than a louder bang emerged from somewhere deeper in the school.

Dracula shrugged. "Don't say he didn't warn us."

I smirked. "Yeah, right. If that's even what it's about."

When we arrived back in the Garden District, one of the three homes had its porch lights on. The windows were also illuminated. The other two houses were pitch black. It made sense to check that house—Garret's house—first.

We got out of the van and walked up the sidewalk toward the house. Delphine put her hand on my shoulder. "Why don't you allow me to speak to them first?"

"Okay. Why?"

Delphine tilted her head. "You're both vampires. If Samuel was here, before, and stole the pendant from them and that's why they were gone and hiding earlier, how do you think they'll react if the first thing they see is the likes of you two? Sienna, you might look like a nice enough girl, but Dracula? Well, you look exactly like everyone thinks you're supposed to look."

"I'm not even wearing my cloak!"

Delphine shook her head. "You still look like yourself."

I smiled. "That's usually what people say about someone when they're looking at a corpse in a casket. Gee, he sure looks like himself."

"I've been in a casket a few times."

"That's the thing," Delphine said. "Dead people in caskets *never* look like themselves. Take the life out of someone, and even the body changes. The point, Dracula, is that your face probably isn't the one they'd most welcome after what they've recently endured. And Sienna, no offense, but you smile too much. When you smile—fangs."

"I can go resting bitch face instead if that helps."

Delphine tilted her head. "That doesn't tend to win friends and influence people. Just let me take the lead on this one. These are old spirits. I'm used to speaking to old spirits."

I sighed. "All right. You make a good point."

I allowed Delphine to walk up ahead of us. Dracula stayed back on the sidewalk while Delphine ascended the four marble stairs that led up the porch between two white Corinthian columns.

She pressed the doorbell.

With my enhanced hearing, I picked up on the sound of footsteps approaching the door. The lock clicked and the door swung open. "May I help you?"

Delphine nodded. "Are you Garret Schumer?"

"I am."

Delphine extended her hand. When Garret shook it, he gasped.

"What's wrong?" Delphine asked.

"Nothing. Your touch. It tingles. It must be my circulation. Apologies."

Delphine smiled. "We're here to talk to you about an item we believe was stolen from you or one of your friends. We'd also like to talk to you about the man who took it."

"Who are you!" Garret shouted. "How do you know about that!"

"What is it, dear?" a tall curly-haired blonde woman of around forty approached.

"Nothing, Leslie. I'll handle this."

"Are Mitchell and Daniel with you?" Delphine asked.

"How do you know our names?" Garret demanded.

Delphine raised her hand as if seeing her palm might calm

him down. He looked right past it and saw Dracula and me. He gasped and took a step back.

"They won't hurt you. They're not like the man who came before."

"He was no man! Neither are they! Demons!"

"Not demons," Delphine corrected him. "Vampires. But don't judge a monster by its cover. After all, you're not really Garret, are you?"

Garret's jaw dropped. "I've gone by that name for decades."

"But it's not you. Not really."

Garret gulped. "I don't know what you're talking about."

"Garret is in there. Funny, I can sense his spirit. You've got him chained up in your mind. I can't usually detect the spirits of the living, but I suppose, given that you're possessing his body, he's more like the dead than you now, isn't he?"

Garret turned. "Leave us alone."

I ran up and grabbed Garret by the arm. "We aren't here to harm you. In fact, I bet having another soul rattling around inside of you, and a disturbed soul at that, isn't always pleasant."

"I'm not talking about this with any of you."

"What if I said we could help? We could separate the two souls and the poor spirit whose body you stole could finally be put to rest?"

"You don't understand. I had to take this body. You don't know what he did to us."

"Feuerhahn?" I asked.

Garret gulped. "How do you know that name?"

"We know everything," Dracula approached Garret and put his hand on his shoulder. "Almost everything. If you can answer a few questions for us, we're willing to give you new, better, bodies of your own. They can look just the same if you'd like. They'll be healthier, and more importantly, they'll be yours."

"What are you? Gods? No one can do anything like that."

I shrugged. "I've met a few gods. Dicks, mostly. You'd be

surprised. But there are a few good ones, and I have a crystal that I can use to form what's called a golem. A soulless body. If you leave the body you're in, the golem is yours. You can go on living forever if you'd like. Golems don't age, just as the body you possess won't so long as you're within it."

Garret's eyes shifted back and forth. "This sounds too good to be true. How can I trust you?"

"I'll make one for each of you. You and your friends. But you need to tell us about the trinket that the vampire stole from you. Can you do that?"

"All you want is information?" Garret asked.

"A little information for a new body," Delphine confirmed. "I don't know about you, but that sounds like a good trade to me."

"Besides, what do you have to lose?" Dracula pointed out. "You already lost the trinket, right?"

Garret huffed. "We only took it so it wouldn't fall into the wrong hands. You wouldn't believe what that little thing can do."

"I understand what Feuerhahn did to you. I can only imagine how he terrorized you in that asylum."

Garret nodded. "It was a long time ago. I try not to think about it. Mitchell, Daniel, and I have new lives. Technically, Thaddeus and Vernon. My name was Earl. It was a long time ago."

I shook my head. "Let me guess. Feuerhahn decided that Earl had to die. *Na na na na.*"

Delphine backhanded me on the shoulder. "Excuse her."

Garret—Earl—laughed. "I picked up the reference. It was funny. Still, I've gone by Garret far longer than I was ever Earl. I know the name belongs to…him. Still, it's odd to hear my old name."

"I remember those names from the files," Dracula said. "Your deaths were listed in the asylum files as by natural causes related to your conditions."

"I was an alcoholic. That's not what they called it back then.

But I didn't drink after I was committed. Mitchell suffered from hysteria, what they call anxiety nowadays. Daniel was probably schizophrenic, but he hasn't exhibited those tendencies in ages."

I nodded. "You mean Thaddeus and Vernon."

"Right. Sorry. Like I said, it's been a long time."

I reached into my pocket and retrieved the trinket. "So, what can you tell us about the doctor's pendant?"

Garret looked surprised. "Well, I can say for certain that's not it."

"Say what?"

"That's not the trinket that was stolen from us. I don't know where you got that from, but that's not it."

Dracula and I exchanged glances. "Well, shit."

"Is the deal still on the table?" Garret asked.

I nodded. "We still have questions. If this isn't it, the vampire who attacked you before still has it. We still need to know what it can do."

CHAPTER TWENTY-NINE

I expected Garret to invite us in. Instead, he told us to wait a moment. One moment turned into about thirty. I suppose he had a lot of explaining to do. He finally returned with who must have been Mitchell and Daniel—or Thaddeus and Vernon.

"Sorry," Garret said. "We'll go do this at Mitchell's. Our families are very close, but our wives don't know the truth about our past."

I tilted my head. "How can you keep that a secret from your *wives?*"

"How couldn't we?" Mitchell piped up. "It's not something you can just lay on someone and expect them to be okay with it. Hey, honey, just thought you should know that I'm actually dead and that you're marrying a body older than your grandfather's."

I smirked. "All right, good point. Still, that must be hard."

"We lived a long time, just us three, before we all agreed it was time to start families and move on. We've all been married over fifteen years. The truth is so far in the past that it doesn't feel like a lie."

"Except for the fact that you still have troubled souls trapped within each of you," Delphine reminded him. "You can't just ignore that."

"You'd be surprised what you learn to ignore over time," Garret said.

"Don't you feel guilty about that?" I asked. "I mean, you took someone else's body."

"The original Garret, Mitchel, and Daniel were three of the worst cases in the entire asylum. They were catatonic most of the time. When they weren't, they hardly made a lick of sense."

"It hasn't changed much," Mitchell added. "The old Mitchell hardly speaks at all. Every now and then I hear a groan or something, but that's about all there is to it."

"What will happen to them if we leave and get new bodies?" Daniel asked.

Delphine shook her head. "It's impossible to know. This isn't exactly common. They may age at an accelerated rate and die very quickly. Or, they may continue as they were."

"They want to die," Garret said. "At least mine does. He has for a long time."

I took a deep breath. "I don't know if that's something we can just make happen."

"You're vampires," Garret said. "Surely you could."

I sighed. "You don't understand. We aren't like you assume. We don't like to kill."

"Not even me!" Dracula put in. "Despite what you might have heard."

"Sorry," Garret said. "I don't think I caught your name before, sir."

"I am Dracula!"

Garret and the others laughed. "No, really."

"What? I am! The one and only!"

"He's not joking," I assured them. "He's actually older than you three."

Mitchell tilted his head. "Well, I'll be damned. I mean, I hope not. But damn! I thought you were just a story."

I shrugged. "He's more of a sorta-living breathing cliché. But he's not who he used to be in those stories."

"And those stories do not contain the whole truth."

"I'm sure they don't," Garret allowed. "Well, boys. It's been a crazy couple of days."

"Would you like me to make your new bodies now?" I asked.

"You can just do that?" Mitchell asked. "You don't have to grow them in test tubes or something?"

I laughed. "It's not like that. I just have to know what you want your bodies to look like. I suppose you want them just the same, you know, since you have wives who might have a lot of questions otherwise."

"Maybe a few minor alterations," Garret suggested. "Could you give Daniel a bigger penis? He's never been able to satisfy his wife."

Daniel punched Garret on the shoulder. "You're an ass!"

Garret laughed. "I'm joking. Chill."

I smirked. "Anything serious you'd like to modify?"

Garret nodded emphatically. "Less ear hair would be nice. I swear, I trim that shit all the time and it comes back before I realize it."

"Thin out my back hair a bit, too," Michell requested.

"He's right," Daniel put in. "He's like sasquatch."

I smiled. "Won't your wives notice?"

Mitchell shrugged. "I've been considering laser hair removal. This will just save me a few hundred bucks."

"I have a club toe," Daniel added. "Gives me all kinds of trouble. My wife doesn't pay that much attention to my feet. Should be fine to fix."

I never should have asked them if they wanted any modifications. They each had a dozen different things they wanted altered. All small things, but programming those details into an archeus crystal took time. I knew the commands. It was a hassle, but I suppose it was worth it. I was taking notes on my phone.

"All right, I've got it."

"Tell us everything you know about the trinket," Dracula pressed.

"It's very simple, really," Garret reported. "It's sharp on one end. The other side is jagged, as if it was broken off something."

"The doctor had it wrapped in some kind of twine and wore it around his neck," Daniel added. "When we were ghosts, if he touched us with it, it captured us."

"It captured you? Like a prison?" I asked.

Mitchell nodded. "It also glowed like the sun when the doctor held a spirit within it. When he put one of us inside of it, he could tell us to do almost anything. For a day or so it was like we'd lost our will. Even as spirits, after he released us, we had to do what he told us."

I sighed. "I've seen that before. It's the tip of a reaper's scythe."

"A scythe can break?" Dracula asked.

I shrugged. "I don't know. I've never heard of anything like that before. I should call Zoey. She'll know."

"So it didn't repel spirits," Dracula mused. "It just put them under a temporary mind-control spell?"

"Pretty much," Garret confirmed. "After a while, it did repel us. Even though we wanted nothing more than to kill him, fear is just as powerful, if not more, than revenge. When he came, the spirits ran. Not because the trinket forced us to, but because we were afraid he'd take us into it."

"It makes sense," I said. "Samuel must've used it on his father. That's what caused so much angst. It's why Abraham created the poltergeist in the schoolhouse."

"Did you say poltergeist?" Garret asked.

"Right. Do you know something about that?"

The three men exchanged glances. "When a spirit was captured by that thing, new entities often emerged after the spirits were freed. Angry spirits. They weren't human. I don't know what they were."

Delphine sighed. "That explains why there were so many poltergeists in the asylum."

I nodded. "To get rid of a poltergeist we either have to kill it with another poltergeist or we have to free the spirit who made it. The spirit has to move on. If we can get the trinket away from Samuel, eventually, it should free Abraham from his control. My guess is that he has Abraham trapped within it."

"It's no wonder Morty could sense the energy from the trinket. It's a reaper blade. Of course he'd sense it. And remember, Morty only sensed it when Samuel called the spirit of the doctor back out of his old body, out of the rat."

"That's also when Alexander and Reginald showed up. My guess is they're the ones holding the trinket right now. At least they were at the time."

"Then what is the significance of the trinket that Samuel gave you?" Dracula asked.

"He must have got it from the Scholomance. Ennigaldi gave it to him. If he failed her, though, why?"

Dracula shook his head. "Maybe he didn't fail Sin. Perhaps he was just one piece of the puzzle to reunite the paths. You are the other."

"I'm not sure if that's a good thing or a bad thing."

Garret cleared his throat. "So I take it you got the info you needed, right? Can I get my new body now?"

CHAPTER THIRTY

I called Zoey's phone, and Kevin, her fiancé, answered. He told me she couldn't come to the phone. She was in labor. I wasn't going to bother her with twenty questions about reaper scythes. I told Kevin to give her my love and to call when she was a mama.

I made the golems for MGD. I'd made enough of them over the last couple of years, including during my various world-saving escapades with Zoey, that I was getting good at it. It took about half an hour. We were lucky the crystal had enough energy to make all three. Those things didn't last forever, but with a full charge, a total of four golems was within an archeus crystal's usual capacity.

When the golems were made, the three possessing spirits left the bodies they'd inhabited for decades and jumped into their new meat suits. They gasped for air, then looked each other over and shared a group hug.

"It worked!" Garret exclaimed. "Thank you!"

I turned and looked at their original bodies. Their eyes were open, wide with terror. I wasn't sure what to do with them, but it turned out I wouldn't have to worry about it. They aged in front of our eyes. The skin on their bodies went loose and wrinkled, their hair turned white, and their complexions turned gray.

"Hello, Sienna."

"Morty?" I turned and hugged him. It was awkward because he was holding his scythe.

"Three additions to the schedule. I figured given the location, it couldn't be a coincidence."

As the spirits within the bodies rose from their frames, Morty caught them each with his scythe. His scythe started to glow.

"That's it!" Garret shouted. "That's the same glow the doctor's trinket had."

"What is he talking about?" Morty asked.

I took a deep breath. "We believe the doctor's trinket was part of a reaper's scythe."

Morty gulped. "I see. That would explain why my father sensed its energy. Why I did, too."

"Refresh my memory. Your dad didn't exactly *see* the trinket, did he?"

"He said it was tucked under the doctor's shirt. He didn't get a good view."

I sighed. "Well, that tracks. Can a scythe be broken like that?"

Morty nodded. "The scythe is a part of a reaper's soul. We're born with the magic that makes it. A scythe can be broken if someone kills a reaper."

I gulped. "Who could kill a reaper? I mean, I know Zoey's ex was killed by a vampire."

"We're not immortal," Morty clarified. "We age and usually ascend to a higher plane. We can live for centuries, though. Our bodies are not invulnerable. It's extremely rare for a human to kill a reaper. It's happened once, maybe twice, ever."

"Maybe twice? You'd think something like that would be well-established in reaper lore."

"The second one was killed by Achilles. He wasn't exactly, totally, human. So the second is a sort of, maybe, human kill."

"Achilles from the Trojan War? Helen of Troy and all that?"

Morty nodded. "Exactly. It's said that even after Paris struck him with the arrow he fought off his first reaper. He killed him and shattered his scythe with a sword. This is basic history taught at the Reaper Academy. We all know it."

"What happened to the remnants of the scythe?"

"No one knows. Probably buried in the ruins of Troy."

Garret cleared his throat.

I turned to him, annoyed. "Sorry, you're free to leave if you'd like. Thanks again."

"No," Garret said. "I had something to say. Doctor Feuerhahn was fascinated with ancient antiquities. His office was full of them. In some of our sessions, you know, before he fried my brain, he insisted that many of them had magical properties. Healing properties, even. He bragged he had the most unique collection in the world and that if we cooperated, if we submitted to his treatments, he'd be able to help us in ways no one has been able to in thousands of years."

I shook my head. "So he was a whack-a-doodle, himself. We already knew that. Garret, when you possess someone, can you access their memories?"

Garret nodded. "Sure can. It goes both ways."

I nodded. "What if the doctor possessed Samuel? It wasn't Samuel's plan, but he made the best of it. He knew Feuerhahn's memories, which was why he was able to appear and even act a lot like the doctor when we found him as a ghost at the asylum. A lot of what Samuel told us about what the doctor was doing may have been the honest truth."

Morty nodded. "It would also be how Samuel learned to use the remnants of the scythe."

"If you take a spirit in your scythe and release it, will it obey you for a time?"

Morty nodded. "Of course. It's how we can ensure that when

we release souls to the boatman they won't try to flee before they're delivered to the afterlife."

Dracula came over. He had been busy wrapping up the bodies with Delphine, Mitchell, and Daniel. "Now that you know what the trinket is, is there a way you might be able to track it?"

Morty grinned. "Most reapers couldn't. Thankfully, I'm not most reapers. Any reaper under my command, I can find. If the shard of the scythe is still out there, it's technically the remnant of a dead reaper. It's alive, in a way. If we're right, that the shard came from the reaper that Achilles killed, I can find out what his name was. Then I can use my scythe to track it down."

I tilted my head. "If that's true, why didn't the Grim Reaper do that after Achilles killed the reaper?"

"The reaper hadn't harvested. His scythe was dormant. Now that we know it's been used, I can find it. I can take you to Samuel."

CHAPTER THIRTY-ONE

We drove back to the schoolhouse. Morty had to return to the underworld to drop off the souls of the original MGD—the dead asylum patients, not the beer—and do some digging to find out the name of the reaper Achilles had killed during the Trojan War. Those were old records, dating back to a time before even his father had been the Grim Reaper. They weren't in his files, but they were in old archives. He insisted it wouldn't take *too* long, and I was hoping it was before nightfall if only because I didn't want to have to worry about the werewolves while we were hunting Samuel.

We needed them. To get to Samuel, we'd have to fight him *and* his equally immortal brothers. I didn't want to put Dylan and his pack in danger, but Dracula and I couldn't handle the Van Helsings alone. We weren't going to bring Delphine with us. She might have been a medium, but she was mortal.

When we got back to the schoolhouse I found Dylan with a broom in his hand near the entrance. Dracula was about to disarm the traps again but Dylan raised his hand.

"Don't bother. This damned poltergeist keeps setting them off. It's making a real mess of the place."

I could hear banging in the distance. It was constant, until Dracula and I stepped inside. Then everything went silent.

I bit my lip. "Well, apparently it likes it when we're here."

I grabbed another broom and helped Dylan clean up. Shattered glass, mostly. The windows in the place were blown out with very few exceptions.

"Very strange behavior for a poltergeist," Delphine noted. "Makes one wonder what exactly old Abraham was so anxious about when he manifested it."

I shook my head. "Unless we get to Samuel and release Abraham so we can ask him, there's no way to know."

We nearly had the whole place cleaned up. Replacing the windows was going to have to wait. Dracula would pay for it, of course. He always did.

The sun was getting low on the horizon. We had maybe an hour before sunset. It meant the wolves might shift. It also meant I wouldn't be as strong. I was still formidable at night, but no more than the average vampire. Under sunlight, I had an advantage. As a daywalker, it made me strong. We were cutting it close.

I was starting to worry when a golden portal showed up and Morty jumped through it. "The reaper was named Myles. I can track the shard."

"All right, everyone!" I called. "It's showtime! Let's load up in the van."

Morty stopped me. "Probably not necessary. They're only a couple blocks away."

I snorted. "Seriously? All this time and they were in the neighborhood?"

Morty shrugged. "Looks like it."

"All right everyone! Go grab some weapons out of the van! Except for you, Delphine."

Delphine raised both hands. "I'm not a fighter, but if you give me the keys, I'll stay in the van at a distance. If Abraham Van

Helsing is in Samuel's thrall, I might be able to help wrest him free if the power from the shard fades."

"Samuel Van Helsing is not a reaper," Morty said. "If I can touch the shard for even a second I can take over control. There may be another option available. The shard isn't so much a piece of a blade but of Myles' soul. If you can deal a mortal blow to Samuel *while he is wearing the shard*, it will harvest his soul."

"A soul containing a soul," Delphine remarked. "That's fascinating."

Morty nodded. "It's our superpower. It's why the shard can control a spirit. We subdue souls. That's what we do. Unlike the doctor before, and Samuel now, we don't do it for our own purpose. We don't *enslave* them. We subdue them that we might give them peace. What Feuerhahn did and Samuel is doing is an abomination. If we get a chance to harvest his soul, I can assure you, he'll receive a one-way trip to Hades."

The plan was simple. I'd go astral and attempt to take out Samuel before his brothers were privy to what I was doing. Dracula and the wolves would come in to fight Alexander and Reginald. Dracula would come in first and try to hold them off while I still had the advantage of fighting with sunlight. Once the sun set, and hopefully the wolves wolfed out, they'd come in and assist Dracula or me—whoever needed the most help.

That was plan A, anyway. If they had those lamps that disrupted my ability to go astral, I'd still go in on one side of the building while Dracula and the wolves faced them head-on. They'd go in first. When the Van Helsings were distracted, I'd go through the wall and take Samuel from behind. The problem was that we wouldn't know if my brooch would work until we were inside—which meant the plans both had to start the same way. Dracula goes in first. I go in next. If we knew for *certain* that they didn't have the lamps, I'd go in first because I'd have the element of surprise, but we had to assume they'd neutralize my astral abilities. These were Van Helsings. They knew who they were facing, even if they didn't know we were coming.

Abraham Van Helsing was a wild card. So long as Samuel could manipulate his father's ghost, his Scholomance power could match Dracula's. In terms of pure magic, they had the advantage. Samuel embraced the path of darkness. I'd taken Ennigaldi's invitation to decline the dark path and promised I'd pursue the united lunar path. I was supposed to be able to access some of those powers, as I did in my vision in the Scholomance, but I hadn't figured out how to make it work on Earth. This wasn't the time to experiment.

Dracula and I threw on chain-mail vests and covered them with leather coats. We were the vegans of supernatural war, stake—steak?—resistant.

Morty led the way. He could go astral too, provided the Van Helsings didn't have the lamps to neutralize that. We had to get him the shard, somehow, some way.

The Van Helsings were in an old defunct Methodist church a couple of blocks away from the schoolhouse. It wasn't a large church. It had a few stained glass windows which, to my chagrin, minimized the amount of sunlight that passed through.

This was a battle we stood a better chance of winning if we made progress fast. A long, drawn-out battle would work to the Van Helsings' advantage, especially if the wolves didn't shift after the sun went down.

The odds of them shifting again were just better than average, but not enough to hinge our plan on it. Not to mention, the Van Helsings had silver bullets. Even after the wolves shifted, *if* they shifted, they were vulnerable. That meant, while I focused on Samuel and tried to get the shard to Morty, Dracula's priority was to neutralize the Van Helsings' weapons. They probably had silver blades as well as silver bullets.

"Be careful," Delphine cautioned. "Fight like hell and come back alive."

I gave Delphine a hug and kissed Dylan on the cheek. "This might be our best shot. It isn't our *only* shot. If things get too bad, don't sacrifice yourselves. Morty can portal us out of there if we need to regroup. Our chances of coming at them again improve if all of us are still breathing."

"Agreed," Dracula put in. "But as you said, this is the best opportunity we have, since they don't know we're coming. I'm confident I can handle the Van Helsing brothers with my power intact."

I nodded. "And so long as I'm still invigorated by sunlight, I like my chances against Samuel. Nothing is guaranteed."

"We'll be ready," Dylan said. "The second we shift, we'll be in to fight."

CHAPTER THIRTY-TWO

I touched my brooch and moved invisibly around to the back of the church. Technically, It was the front of the church's chancel. There weren't a lot of rooms off the main sanctuary. Dracula, meanwhile, was prepared to kick in the front doors and, with a sword in hand, go after Alexander and Reginald.

We didn't have radios or anything like that to coordinate. We relied on our enhanced hearing. Vampires and werewolves alike have acute senses.

I heard a bang that was Dracula's boot against the front double doors. He was fast, and he was good with a blade. Unless the Van Helsings hung out with weapons in their hands all the time, he had a chance to do some damage fast. It was to my advantage to move in immediately before Samuel could arm up as well.

I touched my brooch and passed through the wall under a large stained glass window. My body immediately went corporeal. No surprise. They had lamps to nullify my astral abilities.

Dracula was already on Alexander Van Helsing, and Reginald was gathering weapons. I couldn't worry about that. I charged after Samuel.

Samuel raised a hand and hit me with a concussive blast of black, smoky magic, but I dug in my feet and held my position as the magic blasted me like a hurricane. Even with my enhanced strength, it took everything I had to take a step forward, then another.

Samuel was smiling. "Do you still have your pendant?"

I nodded. "Damn straight."

"Why don't you use it?"

I winced, still fighting against his blast. "Clearly that's what you want me to do. I'm not an idiot."

Samuel laughed and grabbed the shard which was hanging from a piece of twine around his neck. "Stand down, Sienna. Or I'll make sure that my father gets his chance to move on."

"What are you talking about?"

"My father's tether to this world is Dracula. He might have been a wise sage, a master of the Scholomance in the void. On earth, he's a vengeful spirit. In his life, there was one goal he never achieved."

"Killing Dracula." I took another step forward.

Dracula was still fighting against the Van Helsings. He'd knocked Alexander into an oak pew with a punch, and Alexander was struggling to get to his feet. Meanwhile, Reginald met Dracula's blade with his own.

Samuel nodded. "That's right."

"If you release your father, he can't do your bidding. You wouldn't loosen his tether in the middle of the fight."

"Wouldn't I? I don't know, Sienna. I'd still have control of my father until a reaper harvests him, and you'd be down your strongest ally. How much longer can you last with your strength? It's getting dark out there."

I took a deep breath. When I did, some of Samuel's magic flowed into me. It made me stronger. Scholomance power and daywalker power combined. I clenched my hand around the hilt of my sword and pressed my feet against the marble floor of the old church to pick up my speed.

Samuel's eyes widened as I lifted my sword and took a swing at his neck. My strike missed. It hit a cloud of black smoke.

"Shit!"

Samuel reappeared on the opposite side of the room, just behind Dracula. He touched the shard and a white spirit flowed out of it. It wasn't entirely solid, but I recognized the shape. It had just enough definition that I could make out his face. It was Abraham Van Helsing.

The ghost of Abraham blasted into Dracula's body, and the count went stiff and dropped his sword.

Then his eyes glowed gold. Dracula cracked his knuckles. He looked around the room. His face was blank.

"Go after the daywalker!" Samuel commanded.

Dracula turned to me with a wide grin on his face. It wasn't Dracula. Samuel hadn't used Abraham to kill him. Not yet.

Dracula was possessed by Abraham Van Helsing, and Abraham was still in Samuel's thrall.

Reginald tossed Dracula a stake. He caught it and charged after me.

All I could do was try to dodge his attack and hope, if he hit his mark, my chain mail would stop the stake. I wasn't going to kill him. I hadn't known him all that long but in a short time, he'd become a father to me.

"Fight this!" I shouted. As Dracula's daywalker sire, he should listen to me, even when possessed. "Both of you can fight this!"

Samuel laughed. "You think my father wants to resist my influence?"

I nodded. "He isn't an ass like you! I know him!"

The Van Helsing brothers exchanged glances and laughed.

Dracula's eyes flickered. He was resisting Abraham's control.

"Kill me, Sienna!"

"No!"

"Kill me before I kill you!"

"There's one thing you could do," Samuel suggested. "Use the Babylonian trinket. Claim the power of the moon. It won't work for me. It will work for you."

"I don't know what it will do. I'm not taking your bait!"

Samuel shook his head. "I hoped you'd do it yourself. Still, you're wearing it. It'll work just the same."

I grabbed the trinket, still hanging around my neck.

"*Dalamu!*" Samuel screamed.

The pendant burned in my hand as I ripped it off my neck and threw it onto the floor.

It burned red.

Dracula, still fighting Abraham's influence, took a step back.

"What is happening?" I shouted.

"Dalamu is Akkadian," Samuel shot back. "What do you think it means?"

"This isn't a fucking pop quiz, asshole."

Samuel laughed. "It's their word for hell! The place of torment. The prison of the demons!"

"What are you talking about?"

"It didn't respond to me. I didn't pass Ennigaldi's test. Still, I managed to escape with the pendant. Why do you think she wanted *you* to kill me? So you could take the pendant and open the gates of hell, so you could free the demons. And how about that? You just did it!"

"Why would she want to do that? She said she made vampires to fight demons!"

Samuel laughed. "Why do you think? The Babylonians were conquerors. They believed glory could only be earned in battle. Their gods are empowered when their vampires fight. They didn't want you to defeat the demons. They wanted their war so they could come to power!"

"I don't believe you! That's crazy talk!"

"Is it? You were the key. The pendant was the door. I couldn't unlock it."

"I saw you use it before! Back in the schoolhouse!"

"Deception. The pendant of Sin did nothing. It glowed a little when I spoke the word. My brothers used the reaper shard to command the ghost of the doctor out of the rat-shaped body."

I shielded my eyes as red energy overwhelmed the pendant. It melted into the floor and formed a large swirling pool of what looked like magma.

Seven black entities shot out of it and blasted through the stained glass windows and into the world.

"What the hell was that?"

Samuel shrugged. "Demons. What do you think?"

"Why would you do that? You didn't want to fight their war. You failed Ennigaldi's test. You refused Sin!"

"I don't intend to fight in that war," he replied. "Not as a vampire. Thank you for the new body by the way. While you and your kind are caught up fighting devils, I can resume my efforts to take over the world."

A little sunlight poured through the windows on the west side of the church. It was enough to give me extra strength.

Dracula was frozen in place as he fought Abraham as best he could.

"Father!" Samuel shouted. "Use the vampire. Stop her!"

Dracula clenched his fists. "You forgot one thing, son! Abraham and I might be mortal enemies. At least we were. But we're both masters of the path of light!"

The last beams of sunlight from the windows faded. Samuel held out his hand again and shot me with another blast of smoky wind.

Dracula extended both his hands. One of his eyes glowed. The other remained dark. Dracula and Abraham were working together. They were fighting Samuel's influence.

Light flickered from Dracula's hands. He was trying to give

me more power. More strength. Samuel clutched the shard. "Stop it! I commanded you!"

"Looks like that power in that shard is waning." I smirked.

"Alexander! Reginald!" Samuel screamed.

"You unleashed devils!" Alexander fired back. "You want us to help you? What the hell is wrong with you?"

"Take the shard from him!" I screamed.

Alexander looked incredulous. "We're not helping you, either, vampire. Come on, Reggie. Let's get out of here."

"You can free your father!"

Alexander turned back as he and his brother headed for the door. "Our father is dead."

When the Van Helsing brothers opened the double doors, Dylan, Logan, and Ian came bounding in on all fours. They'd shifted. All three of them jumped on Samuel, snarling, as Alexander and Reginald left, shaking their heads.

A blast of black power sent the wolves flying and crashing into the walls. They gave me enough of a window that I ran right up to Samuel without resistance. He extended his hand to catch my neck and reached to his belt and retrieved a stake.

"It's a shame it had to end this way, Sienna. We could have made a great team when I took over the world. But once again, you're short-sighted."

A golden glow appeared behind Samuel. Morty jumped out and ripped the shard off Samuel's neck. It glowed in Morty's hand.

Samuel's eyes widened in shock. A blast of white light hit me from behind as Dracula and Abraham poured all the light-path power they had into me.

I kicked Samuel in the balls and he buckled over.

"Yeah, it's a shame you had to be such an ass. You could have helped me save the world."

Morty raised the shard over his head. When he did, Abraham's ghost blasted out of Dracula and struck his own son.

Light poured out of Samuel's eyes, his nostrils, his ears, and his wide-open mouth.

Samuel's body exploded in sunlight. His spirit hovered in the air, a red, twisty, ethereal form.

Morty took his scythe, swung it, and harvested Samuel.

When he was done, Abraham stood where his son had been. He glowed with white and gold power, like an angel.

"You killed your own son?"

Abraham shook his head. "That wasn't my son. Not anymore. I saved him from himself."

"You saved us!" Tears fell down my cheeks. Dracula stepped up behind me and placed a hand on my shoulder.

"Thank you, old friend."

Abraham laughed. "Old friend?"

Dracula shrugged. "Times change, right?"

"They certainly do. Samuel was my tether, not you. I was so disturbed by his behavior at the Scholomance I came here with one mission: to attempt to stop him. I didn't foresee that he'd come upon a shard of a reaper's scythe."

"You left a poltergeist at the schoolhouse. What was that about?"

Abraham smiled. "I hoped to warn you. I learned what Samuel intended to do. How he intended to open the gate to hell and release the demons. I hoped my angst, my poltergeist, might stop you from coming here. At least until you figured out what was happening and could destroy the Babylonian pendant."

I took a deep breath and exhaled. "Poltergeists don't have the best communication skills."

Abraham bowed his head. "It was a desperate hope to slow you down. I didn't expect it would work. However, now that my son is gone, I can rest in peace."

"Back to the Scholomance?" I asked.

Abraham shook his head. "That's not my personal heaven anymore. Not now that Sin has taken over."

"Are you ready to go?" Morty asked.

"Don't put me in that scythe with Samuel."

Morty held up the shard. "I can use this instead."

Abraham nodded. "Then I'm almost ready. There are a few things more I must say." He turned to me. "If I could hug you, I would. You changed me, Sienna. That time we spent together in the Scholomance. You taught me that not every vampire is a monster. You helped me release my anger, my rage, toward vampires. Including Dracula."

"You're a good man, Abraham."

"I appreciate you saying so. Herein lies your next challenge. Seven deadlies have emerged from hell."

"Seven deadlies? You mean demons?"

"The seven deadly sins. You've met Sloth before."

I nodded. "Yeah, he doesn't do much."

"Don't underestimate what he can do now that he's on Earth. Imagine if he spread his sloth through the world. Absolute sloth. People refusing to do so much as get up to eat or get a glass of water."

I shuddered. "I didn't realize Sloth could be so deadly."

"You must also face six others, each a deadly demon in their own right. Pride, Greed, Lust, Envy, Gluttony, and Wrath."

"I'm supposed to use this lunar power, the reunited paths, to fight them."

"That's what Ennigaldi and Sin want you to do. When you fight them, you empower them. You'll have to find another way. If you use the power of the Scholomance—and I imagine it's only a matter of time now that my son is dead that you'll be fully vested in those abilities—any demon you kill with those skills will strengthen Sin. It will make him stronger than the other gods. Strong enough to kill them."

I gulped. "How can I kill a demon without using magic? I'm just a vampire."

Abraham shook his head. "Not true. You're a *daywalker*. And you have friends who might help."

I looked over and saw the three werewolves huddled in a corner. Dylan was focused on keeping Logan and Ian in check.

I bit my lip. "I can't use those powers to fight the demons, I get that. Does that mean I can't use those powers at all?"

"It does not. So long as you do not use those powers in battle, you should be fine."

"So I can use the lunar power to resist the effects of a werewolf's bite, right?"

Dracula laughed. "Romance is in the air."

Abraham smiled widely. "You certainly can."

"Is there anything else you can tell me about how to fight these demons?" I asked.

Abraham shook his head. "All I know is the little I was able to pick up during my time in the Scholomance. There was a surprisingly large amount of reference material on demons there. I never knew why until I learned of the true origins of the paths. Suffice it to say, I know how dangerous those demons can be but I don't know how or when they will attack. Somehow, you'll have to bind them back in hell where Athena can control them again."

Dracula took a deep breath. "I hate to suggest it. I know she has a lot on her plate. But it sounds to me like you're going to need to team up with your friend, again. She's the only one I know of who can send a demon to hell. Her scythe will reap them back to Athena, provided we can find the seven deadlies in time."

I nodded. "We need to go see Zoey. I'd like to meet her baby. The last thing I want to do is ask a new mother to go to war. Still, if the fate of the world depends on it, if Sin could murder the other gods, including her father, she'll fight with me. We'll fight side-by-side one last time."

I smiled at Abraham. "Thank you again. For everything. I know it must've been hard to do what you did. I'm sorry Samuel couldn't be saved."

Abraham nodded. "There's no saving his soul. But perhaps we've saved him already. We've saved him from becoming the monster he never wanted to be."

Morty stepped in front of Abraham. "Are you ready?"

Abraham nodded. "I am."

Dracula smiled at his old nemesis. "Van Helsing. Rest in peace."

CHAPTER THIRTY-THREE

Delphine was waiting for us in the van. She already knew what had happened. She sensed Van Helsing's spirit the moment he was free. Now that he was gone, his poltergeist would be gone as well.

Getting Dylan and the other wolves back to the schoolhouse in the middle of the night wasn't going to be easy. I decided to stay at the church with them. So far as I knew, Zoey was still in labor. Morty said he'd come back and portal us there to see her later after he dropped off Samuel and Abraham with the boatman.

Dracula spent a few moments with me to help me figure out how to wield my new power. The moment the Babylonian pendant opened the portal to hell, I'd felt a change. So much was going on that I wasn't sure if it was adrenaline or something more. Now that it had been a while and my heart rate had returned to normal, which, for a vampire, is about five beats per minute, I knew the sensation was more than that. It was the combined power of the light and dark paths. The power of the moon, the power of Sin.

I knew what they wanted me to do. They wanted me to raise

up more vampires like me. To bring them into the lunar path, to become an army of vampires to fight the demons. Ennigaldi and Sin didn't care so much if I won or lost, the best I could figure. They only wanted the power they'd gather if I used my power to kill the demons. The seven deadly sins. I wasn't so sure now whether the name Sin was pure coincidence or not.

All I had to do to thwart the paralyzing effects of a werewolf's bite—or his other fluids—was to allow the magic to flow freely through my body. I was pretty sure that was already happening.

Of course, it wasn't like I was going to shack up with Dylan during a full moon. I might be freaky, but I ain't *that* freaky. Still, once he was back in human form, it was game on. Once we had a moment of privacy, at least. And probably not in the church. I'm not exactly a superstitious chick, and the taboo aspect of it was mildly appealing, but even I couldn't bring myself to do the dirty there. There are some lines one shouldn't cross. Still, the desire was there. Pent up for months. I didn't need the deadly sin, the demon of lust, to coax me into it.

The wolves were docile under Dylan's influence, and I sat with my back against a wall as Dylan rested his large furry head in my lap. I scratched him behind the ears. Being in a relationship with a werewolf can get weird. How many girls scratch their boyfriends behind the ears or rub their bellies while saying "good boy"?

Maybe more than I realized. People do strange things. I've been on the Internet. I've been in chat rooms with horn balls who had all kinds of weird ideas. Still, it didn't feel odd to comfort Dylan that way while he was a werewolf. It was comforting for both of us.

It was nice to just sit and do nothing for a while. Knowing that seven demons were out there, each representing the worst of humanity's temptations, was unsettling. Still, until we knew what they were doing or how we'd fight them, I could do nothing but sit, rest, and snuggle with a cuddly werewolf boyfriend.

I was thirsty. I could have used a bottle of blood. Thankfully, we had plenty waiting for us back at the schoolhouse. Nothing's better than a good O-negative for breakfast. Better than bacon, if you happen to be a vampire.

We sat there until sunrise. I didn't have to sleep, but I might have dozed off once or twice for a few minutes at a time. Dylan had shifted back into human form while his naked body lay in my lap. I stroked his hair.

"Good morning, sunshine."

Dylan scratched behind his ear. I laughed.

"Sorry. Force of habit."

I chuckled. "Where are your clothes?"

Dylan sighed. "We had to shift outside, and since we weren't a hundred percent sure we *would* shift, we didn't strip down on the sidewalk. Now I wish we had. How are we going to go back home?"

I smiled. "Looks like we're going streaking!"

"You're going to go naked with us?" Dylan smirked.

I grabbed Dylan by the back of his hair and pulled him into a deep kiss. "No, honey. But I'll follow close behind and enjoy the view."

"You kissed me!"

I smiled. "I have the power now. We can be together."

Dylan's eyes widened. He kissed me again, without any hesitancy. "I love you!"

I smiled. "Love you too, puppy."

CHAPTER THIRTY-FOUR

There's something inherently hilarious about seeing three young men run naked, their family jewels firmly cupped in their hands, across two city blocks. I didn't even try not to laugh, especially when someone drove by and honked their horn.

We were in New Orleans, not far from the French Quarter. It wasn't the first time anyone had woken up in a compromising unclothed situation.

We managed to get back to the schoolhouse without encountering the police, and the schoolhouse doors were open when we arrived. We ran inside, the wolves with more urgency than me.

No banging. No glass breaking or flying objects. It worked. Abraham Van Helsing was at rest and so was his poltergeist.

The wolves went to their rooms to get dressed, and I found Dracula with Delphine in the cafeteria. Dracula had a wineglass in front of him with a small amount of blood in the bottom. He picked it up and swirled it around before he tossed me a bottle. I twisted my thumb into the cork and opened it.

Two other men I hadn't noticed stood as I raised the bottle to my lips. It was Alexander and Reginald Van Helsing.

"What the hell are you two doing here?"

"We want to help. For the sake of our father."

I shook my head. "I don't know."

"Hear them out," Dracula urged. "You were the one telling me all this time that Abraham could be trusted. We should give his sons a chance."

"You left and said you couldn't help a vampire."

Reginald sighed. "We were wrong."

"You weren't the one who said it."

"*I* was wrong," Alexander added. "We weren't entirely absent. We listened to what happened from outside the church doors. If these demons are going to unleash hell on Earth, we can't stand by and let it happen."

I nodded. "Well, we could use your help. Especially when it comes to tracking these bastards down."

"We also know a few things about fighting demons," Reginald offered. "There have been times when under the thrall of the former King of Hell, the demons have come to Earth. I'm not sure if it was these particular seven deadlies, but we've fought demons before."

"You have methods to stop them?"

"Holy water. Exorcisms. Demons can't do much without a host. They can afflict a few people here or there, but they're much more powerful when they possess someone. That's also when they're most vulnerable."

I scratched the back of my head. "All right. We do need your help. But if you even *think* about turning on us, I'll remove your heads. Got it?"

Alexander smiled. "I'd like to keep my head. I'm sort of attached to it."

Dracula slapped his knee, laughing. "That's hilarious! I'll have to remember that one!"

I rolled my eyes. "Then it's a deal. First things first, though, I need to pay Zoey a visit. I'm not doubting your capabilities, boys, but she can reap demons. More efficient than an exorcism."

"Perhaps," Alexander allowed. "Like you said, we need all the help we can get. If what my father told you is correct, we also need to be careful. I don't think the Babylonian god is going to sit back and allow us to fight this war without trying to force you to use your powers."

"I know. I won't use those powers. Not unless I don't have any other choice."

"What could force you to make that choice?" Dracula asked.

"If lives are at stake, if it comes down to it, I can't let the demons murder millions of people. All the more reason why we need to act fast and stop these demons the second they turn up."

"We'll start tracking them straight away," Reginald promised. "There are certain signs that will signal the presence of demons in a community. Widespread pestilence, diseased crops, dead herds of cattle. All these things will give us a heads-up that there are demons in an area and give us a chance to act."

"We may need Morty's help so we can travel," Dracula suggested. "I doubt these demons are going to limit their activities to the greater New Orleans area."

"Speak of the devil! Well, not the devil. Speak of the Grim Reaper, anyway!"

I turned and saw Morty standing at the door to the cafeteria. He wasn't in his cloak anymore, and he wasn't holding his scythe.

"You're back! Everything go well?" I asked.

Morty nodded. "Athena is in a panic. She managed to close the portal from the other side, but not before the seven deadly demons escaped."

I sighed. "Well, it's a good thing she stopped the rest of her legions from getting through."

"Seven demons is still more than enough to destroy the world," Alexander pointed out. "But you're right. It could have been worse."

"Have you checked your phone?" Morty asked.

I reached into my pocket. My phone was dead. "I haven't. My battery died overnight."

"I was back in Kansas City before I came. The baby is here!"

"Is it a boy or a girl?" I asked.

Morty laughed. "I'm not supposed to say. Zoey's excited for Auntie Sienna to come and meet her new niece."

"You weren't supposed to say!"

Morty tilted his head and dropped his jaw. "Damn it. Me and my fat mouth."

I chuckled. "No worries. I'll act surprised."

CHAPTER THIRTY-FIVE

I left with Morty. Dracula and everyone else stayed behind. We didn't want to overwhelm Zoey, Kevin, and the baby with too many visitors.

We appeared in Zoey's and Kevin's house.

"Not in the hospital?" I asked.

Morty shook his head. "They didn't make it to the hospital. The doula called over a midwife and they delivered the baby at home."

"Damn. No epidural or painkillers. That's hardcore."

"My sister is a badass. What can I say?"

I chuckled. "Trust me. I know."

I followed Morty to the master bedroom, where Zoey and Kevin were both sitting in bed. Zoey was nursing her baby girl.

"Sienna!" Zoey's face widened with excitement when she saw me. "You look like hell!"

I laughed. "It was a long night."

"Tell me about it!"

"But you look amazing!"

"Thanks! Want to hold your niece?"

"It's a girl! Yay!"

Zoey tilted her head and shot daggers from her eyes at Morty. She knew me too well. I couldn't pretend with her. "You told her?"

"It slipped! Sorry!"

I laughed. "I'm excited. What's her name?"

Zoey handed the baby to me. I cradled her in her arms. "Meet Josephine."

"Aw! You named her after your mom!"

Zoey nodded. "I did."

"She's so fucking cute!"

"Language!" Zoey piped up. "There's a child present."

I laughed. "Right. I meant, she's cray-cray adorbs!"

"I think she looks like me!" Kevin said.

I rolled my eyes and looked at Zoey, who was shaking her head. "Every father thinks their baby looks like him. She's a mini Zoey, a hundred percent."

I rocked Josephine in my arms and kissed her on the forehead.

"So, Morty said you kicked ass last night."

I chuckled. "That's one way to put it. We might have a problem. I hate to even ask."

"What is it?" Zoey asked.

"You didn't mention anything, Mort?"

He shook his head. "Wasn't the best time to bring up the potential demon apocalypse."

Zoey huffed. "A demon apocalypse?"

I nodded. "The seven deadly sins. You remember Sloth. Well, he has six brothers. And they're all assholes. Sorry, language."

"And Athena can't pull them back to hell?"

I shook my head. "The demons weren't born in hell. They were imprisoned there. These demons are totally free of her influence. It's a long story, but if we don't stop them, they'll wreak havoc all over the world. And if we stop them the wrong way, we'll empower an ancient Babylonian god who has a hard-on for murdering all the other gods and becoming the one and only."

"That means my father…"

I nodded. "It does. All the Olympians. Not to mention, every other god in existence."

Zoey bit her lip. She glanced at Kevin, who nodded. "You need to help."

Zoey smiled widely. "I didn't think you'd agree if I asked."

Kevin laughed. "That's why I didn't let you ask."

"I might need a few days to recover. Do you think you can hold them off until then?"

I nodded. "We don't even know where they are or what they're up to. The Van Helsing brothers are going to track them for us."

"We're teaming up with the Van Helsings?"

"Never thought I'd see the day," I admitted.

"I never thought I'd be a mother!"

"Are you sure you want to do this?" I asked. "Josephine is your priority, now."

Zoey nodded. "She's why I have to do this. If the gods fall, the reapers are next. Josephine will inherit my skills. I'm not going to fight just to save the world. I trust you to handle that. I'm fighting for my baby."

AUTHOR NOTES - THEOPHILUS MONROE

APRIL 13, 2023

This book brought back a lot of old memories. No, I've never teamed up with Dracula to fight the ghost of Abraham Van Helsing.

I did have a brief career as a paranormal investigator. It was about fifteen years ago, back in the heyday of the *Ghost Hunters* television show. I was fascinated with the paranormal and, I suppose, I still am.

I belonged to a small group of high-tech investigators in Ohio. We investigated a "haunted" theater and several homes. I never saw a full-bodied apparition or any worldview-shattering experiences. I was always out to try and disprove any claims. If I could explain the phenomena with a rational explanation, Occam's razor applied. The simplest explanation is usually the right one.

Still, I did collect a handful of EVPs with the voices recording at a frequency that *supposedly* corresponds with paranormal phenomena. When investigating the haunted theater we saw the stage lights flicker on and off while the power was cut off to the light system. A faulty switch, perhaps? The creepiest part of the theater was the consume room where they had a lot of masks, dolls, and other props. Nothing paranormal happened. We captures a lot of "dust" orbs on our infrared cameras, and a few strange and unexplained shadows. That's the thing about shadows, though. Light sources can move and so can people or objects.

While I never found any conclusive evidence during my 2-3 years investigating claims of hauntings and paranormal phenomena, I still learned a lot about the various theories surrounding ghosts/spirits and the like. It was fun to revisit some of those ideas as I was writing this novel.

Like Dracula in this book, I was among the few who ran "toward" strange things rather than away. I've always been curious. Is there more out there that as limited humans we simply can't perceive with our limited senses? Our eyeballs can only capture three dimensions. Physics tells us there are more dimensions that we can't perceive. That means, more likely than not, there's a lot "out there" that we don't see and can't observe with our natural senses. There are things that different animals can perceive that we can't. If I were a betting man (every time I've put money in a slot machine I lost it all) I'd say the chances are better than not that there's more to "reality" than the mechanisms of observation and the scientific method are equipped to prove.

At the very least, pondering the *possibility* of such things gives me a lot of fodder for stories like this one. I hope you enjoyed reading it as much as I enjoyed writing it! We have several more *Daywalker* adventures planned, so stay tuned!

-Theo

AUTHOR NOTES - MICHAEL ANDERLE

APRIL 17, 2023

First, thank you for not only reading this story, but these author notes in the back as well!

Haunted Houses, Ghosts, and Apparitions - Oh my!

Let me start by saying there is absolutely NO way you would find me anywhere near a haunted house, ghosts, or anything remotely like an apparition. The mere thought of it sends shivers down my spine.

Interestingly enough, I'd love to chat with a ghost. Imagine the questions you could ask and the stories they could share!

What if we could find an old ghost and ask them historical questions, gaining insights into the past that we could not obtain from books or research alone? What if we could travel back in time and ask a soul just after they expired questions before they disappeared into the great beyond?

The possibilities are endless and utterly fascinating. The knowledge that could be gained and the mysteries that could be solved are tantalizing to consider.

So, while you won't find me wandering through a graveyard or tiptoeing around a haunted mansion, that doesn't mean I don't find the concept incredibly intriguing. The notion of communicating with the other side opens up a world of wonder and curiosity, one I can't help but explore through my writing.

I hope you enjoy this journey into the unknown as much as I've enjoyed writing it.

Ad Aeternitatem,

Michael Anderle

MORE STORIES with Michael newsletter HERE: https://michael.beehiiv.com/

Scared Shiftless

Bat Shift Crazy

No Shift, Sherlock

Shift for Brains

Shift Happens

Shift on a Shingle

The Vilokan Asylum of the Magically and Mentally Deranged

The Curse of Cain

The Mark of Cain

Cain and the Cauldron

Cain's Cobras

Crazy Cain

The Wrath of Cain

The Blood Witch Saga

Voodoo and Vampires

Witches and Wolves

Devils and Dragons

Ghouls and Grimoires

More to come!

FREE URBAN FANTASY ADVENTURE: DRUIDESS (GET IT HERE!)

GoE OMNIBUS COLLECTIONS [in Chronological Order]:

The Druid Legacy

Wyrmrider (Books 1-4)

The Voodoo Legacy

The Legacy of a Vampire Witch

The Legend of Nyx

The Vilokan Asylum of the Magically and Mentally Deranged

Other Theophilus Monroe Series

<u>**Nanoverse**</u>

[Also Available in an Omnibus Edition]

<u>**The Elven Prophecy**</u>

[Also Available in an Omnibus Edition]

<u>**Chronicles of Zoey Grimm**</u>

[Also Available in an Omnibus Edition]

<u>**The Daywalker Chronicles**</u>

<u>**Go Ask Your Mother**</u>

AS T.R. MAGNUS

<u>**Kataklysm**</u>

Blightmage

Ember

Radiant

<u>**FREE EPIC: DARKWORLD (GET IT HERE!)**</u>

BOOKS BY MICHAEL ANDERLE

Sign up for the LMBPN email list to be notified of new releases and special deals!

https://lmbpn.com/email/

For a complete list of books by Michael Anderle, please visit:

www.lmbpn.com/ma-books/

CONNECT WITH THE AUTHORS

Connect with Theophilus Monroe

Website: www.theophilusmonroe.com

Social Media
https://www.facebook.com/pages/category/Author/
Theophilus-Monroe-Urban-Fantasy-Author-101469961530864/

Connect with Michael Anderle

Website: http://lmbpn.com

Email List: https://michael.beehiiv.com/

https://www.facebook.com/LMBPNPublishing

https://twitter.com/MichaelAnderle

https://www.instagram.com/lmbpn_publishing/

https://www.bookbub.com/authors/michael-anderle